The Outlaw's Bride

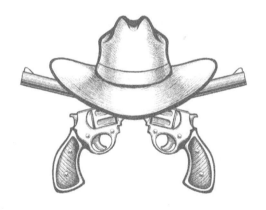

Wyoming Series: Book 1

The Outlaw's Bride

Ruth Ann Nordin

Chapter One

July 1868
South of Laramie, Wyoming

Lillian Christian pulled back the curtain of the stagecoach and noted the mountains all around them.

"Isn't that a beautiful view?" Mildred Washington, who'd told her to call her Millie, asked.

It was nothing like the Atlantic Ocean, but then, this was what Lillian had wanted. Something different. Something new. Something so far removed from her past that she'd never think of Virginia again.

"I'm telling you," Millie continued, "those mountains make you realize just how small we really are in the world."

"Yes, they do." And that was exactly what Lillian was hoping for. Maybe out here, she'd be so small she'd disappear.

Lillian set the curtain back into place and closed her eyes, willing her queasy stomach to settle, though it would do no good. It was so hot and stuffy in the stagecoach, and all of her attempts to secure the curtain in place so that the breeze could keep coming into it had been for nothing. The driver had warned them the stagecoach was old, and he hadn't been exaggerating. It was unfortunate there wasn't a better way to get to Laramie.

She would have stopped off in Cheyenne when she was there if she hadn't answered a mail-order bride ad when she was back in Virginia. Charles Gray was expecting her, and she owed it to him to finish the rest of the journey. Besides, he was a widower with a little boy. She couldn't turn her back on a child who needed a mother. So really, all the swaying of the coach and sticky heat was going to be worth it.

"Are you nervous about meeting your groom?" Millie asked.

"Yes," Lillian admitted. "Are you?"

"Oh, I'm not going to marry anyone. I'm going to Medicine Bow to be a schoolteacher. Schoolteachers aren't allowed to marry until they fulfill their contracts."

Lillian bit her lower lip. Maybe she should have signed a contract to be a schoolteacher. She hadn't even thought of it. She'd only thought of getting a husband. That was a lack of foresight on her part. She'd heard women out West had more freedoms than women who lived back East did. But all of her life, she'd relied on her father and brother to get by, so it felt natural to get a husband.

"I'm sure the man you're going to marry will take one look at you and be glad you came all the way out here to meet him," Millie said. "I love how red your hair is, and your skin is so perfect." She put her hand on Lillian's arm. "I hope you don't mind me saying so, but you look like a porcelain doll that was in the wealthy household my parents worked in. In fact, your hat and dress make me think of that doll, too."

With a frown, Lillian inspected the dark green dress she'd bought in Cheyenne. It was, by no means, as fancy as anything she'd had back East, but it was now occurring to her that it might be much too fancy for living out here. Had she made a mistake by not wearing something like Millie's dress? The woman wore a faded blue dress with flowers printed on it.

Oh dear. Just what had Lillian gotten herself into? Charles was never going to think she was suitable to be a rancher's wife. He might take one look at her and send her right back to Virginia.

The sound of a gunshot rang through the air, bringing Lillian out of her thoughts. "Did you hear that?" she asked Millie.

Millie didn't have time to respond. The stagecoach veered sharply to the left, and Millie ended up pinning Lillian against the window. This was it! The stagecoach was going to tip completely over, and they might suffer injuries because of it. Lillian squeezed her eyes shut and braced herself for impact.

A few more gunshots rang through the air. The stagecoach fell back into place and then came to an abrupt stop. Lillian and Millie lurched forward and hit the other side of the stagecoach. With a grunt, Lillian crumpled to the floor. Millie fell on top of her.

"I'm so sorry," Millie said.

Lillian grabbed her and shushed her. "Don't get up," she whispered. "I think we're being attacked."

Millie gasped, but she kept her voice low. "I heard there were outlaws out in this territory."

Outlaws. Or the man back in Virginia she was supposed to marry. *Oh dear Lord, please don't let it be Robert.*

The gunshots stopped, and she could make out the distinct sound of men shouting. She had to know if Robert was one of them. She had to know if her escape had been in vain. She'd thought she'd covered her tracks, but maybe she'd missed something.

She squirmed from underneath Millie and edged over to the window. After a moment to gather her courage, she peeled back a small portion of the curtain and peeked around it.

"What do you see?" Millie whispered.

"Nothing yet."

"Throw your guns down and no one will get hurt," came a man's voice.

She didn't recognize that voice, so it couldn't be Robert.

She shifted and went to the other side of the window and peeked around that side of the curtain. She finally caught sight of a man on a horse. He had his gun pointed in the direction of the driver and the gunman who were supposed to protect Lillian and Millie from things like this. He wore a bandana over his nose and mouth, and his hat was low over his eyes. So all she had to go on were his red and black plaid shirt and his blue denims to identify him if a lawman asked her questions later on.

"What do you see?" Millie whispered.

"An outlaw," she whispered.

Another outlaw, this one wearing a brown shirt and blue denims, approached the first one. He also had a gun, and his face was also covered. He whispered something to the man in the red and black plaid shirt, and the man nodded. Then, as if he could feel the weight of her stare on him, his gaze went to her.

Gasping, she ducked down and scooted away from the window. Did he know she was watching him?

"What is it?" Millie whispered, huddled next to her. "What did you see?"

"I think one of them saw me," she replied.

"One of them? But I thought you didn't see more than one outlaw out there."

"That was right before another one approached him. I don't know how many there are."

"Look, we don't want any trouble," the man in the red and black plaid shirt called out to the driver and gunman. "Just put the guns down, and no one will get hurt."

"We can't do that," the driver replied. "We got people in the stagecoach to protect."

"One of those people will be better off with us," the man said. "If you know what's good for her, you'll throw down your guns."

4

Good for her? What did that mean? Lillian looked at Millie, but she seemed as confused as Lillian was.

"Just shoot him and get it over with," the man in the brown shirt said, impatience in his voice.

"No," the first outlaw replied. "We're going to do the right thing."

"But no one will believe we did the right thing," the man in the brown shirt argued.

"It doesn't matter if they believe it or not. It's a matter of principle. Once we sink to his level, we'll be no better than a pack of wolves." After a moment, he directed his voice to the driver and gunman. "We only want Lillian Christian. We won't hurt her."

Lillian couldn't have heard them say her name. She was sure she'd heard wrong. Except Millie grabbed her and held onto her as if doing so would guarantee they weren't going to get their hands on her. And that was when she knew she'd heard him just fine.

Did Robert hire them to come for her? Did Robert figure out her alias and hire some men to chase her down? Were they getting paid to kidnap her and take her back to Virginia?

The cocking of a gun echoed through the still air.

"It's not worth it, Jim," the driver told the gunman. "If they wanted to rob us, they would have done it already." He paused then asked, "You mean it? You won't hurt the young woman?"

"You have my word," the outlaw with the red and black shirt promised.

A long moment passed, and then Lillian heard guns being tossed to the ground. Did she dare peek out the window and see what else was going on? Or was it better for her to stay where she was?

The door of the stagecoach opened, making both women jerk back. The outlaw wearing the red and black plaid shirt peered into the small, dark space. Lillian's gaze went to the gun in his holster. He wasn't going to use it on her, was he? Had he meant it when he said that no one would get hurt?

"Which one of you is Lillian Christian?" he asked.

Lillian's gaze went to his face, and since he still had the bandana covering his nose and mouth, she could only make out his blue eyes.

Millie clung tighter to her and didn't utter a peep. Lillian had to admit it was very sweet that this woman, who until recently had been a stranger, was willing to risk everything to protect her.

"Neither one of you will be hurt," he said. "I promise. I just need to get Lillian Christian. Lillian," he glanced from one to the other, "I don't have time to explain, but if you keep riding this stagecoach, you're going to be in a lot of trouble."

Lillian swallowed then forced out, "What kind of trouble?"

He focused in on her. "I take it you're Lillian."

Maybe she shouldn't have been so quick to speak up. Sure, he said he wasn't going to hurt her, but how did she know he meant it?

"Come on!" the second outlaw yelled, making the man glance over his shoulder. "We don't have all day."

"Please, come with me," the man said, turning his attention back to her. "If you don't, then there's likely to be a shootout, and if that happens, I can't guarantee anyone will get out of this alive. I know you have a lot of questions, but I can't explain everything right now. When we're safe, I'll tell you what's going on."

She glanced at Millie who didn't seem to know if either of them could trust him. "Why don't you want Millie? Why does it have to be me?"

"Because you're the one Charles Gray is expecting to marry," he said as he extended his hand to her.

There was no way these men could be from Robert. Robert didn't know anything about her engagement to Charles. She had made sure he didn't find out before she left.

She took a deep breath, wishing there was more time to make this decision. But she could tell by the anxious neighing of the horses that the outlaws were getting restless. She licked her lips. "If I go, you promise no harm will come to Millie, the driver, or the gunman?" she asked.

"Yes. It's not them Charles is after. It's you," he replied.

"You don't know that he's telling the truth," Millie whispered.

"No, I don't. But what if he is?" Lillian whispered in return.

If she went, then she was the only one who would risk being hurt. The others would be safe. If she stayed, who knew what the outlaws would do to them? Sometimes a person had to act on faith, and in this situation, she was just going to have to hope she was making the right decision.

"Alright," she said. "I'll come with you."

"Lillian," Millie pleaded as she pulled Lillian closer to her.

Lillian shrugged Millie away and took the man's hand so he could help her out of the stagecoach. She stepped into the sunlight, and it took her a moment to figure out there were two other outlaws with them, and bandanas were covering most of their faces, too. If these men were the honest type, then why did they hide their faces?

The man next to her pointed to the trunks on top of the stagecoach. "Which is yours?"

So that was it. They came for the trunk since it was the only place she could hide anything of value. "The—" Her voice cracked. She cleared her throat. "The black one."

"That one," he called out to the outlaw wearing the brown shirt. As that outlaw went to get her trunk, the one next to her patted the small of her back. "You're braver than you look."

In the next second, he went over to the other outlaws and helped him secure the trunk to the horse. She let out a shaky breath. She didn't feel very brave right now. The decision hadn't been all that difficult. She was choosing the only way she could think of to protect Millie and the two men who were in charge of the stagecoach. Anyone would do the same thing in her situation.

She glanced over at Millie who mouthed the words that bid her to come back into the stagecoach. She gave a slight shake of her head. No. She'd done enough running. If this was where things went bad for her, then so be it. She couldn't run forever. And if she could save others in the process, then her sacrifice wouldn't be in vain.

The outlaw with the red and black plaid shirt returned to her. "You'll ride with me." He took her by the arm and led her to his horse.

"Charles Gray won't stand for this," the driver called out.

"We'll deal with Charles later," the man replied, not the least bit disturbed by the warning. "You tell him if anyone's to be afraid, it's him."

"You don't know who you're messing with," the driver argued.

"We know exactly who we're messing with," the man muttered under his breath. He helped her onto the saddle and then got up behind her.

She grabbed the saddle horn so she wouldn't fall off, but in one swift motion, he wrapped his arm around her waist, securing her to him. Then he lifted the reins and snapped them.

With one accord, the group of outlaws headed away from the stagecoach, leading her to an entirely different future than the one she'd thought she was going to have when she agreed to be Charles' mail-order bride.

Chapter Two

Mic Gray hated scaring Lillian Christian the way he had. He didn't know anything about her except what his sister, Abby, had told him. A month ago when he'd been in town, Abby said Charles had arranged for Lillian to come out here to be his mail-order bride.

He couldn't sit idly by and let it happen. Abby had been on board with the idea of rescuing Lillian when he suggested it. His brother, Wade, and their friend, Jeremiah, on the other hand had been more reluctant to do so. But they were all here, heading for the mountains that would take them to his cabin, and that was all that mattered.

Lillian was quiet during the ride. But so was everyone else for that matter. He almost removed the bandana because the thing made breathing almost impossible, especially in the sweltering heat, but he didn't dare. Not yet. Not until it was safe to stop and take a break. They had all agreed to keep on riding until they reached the abandoned cabin just south of the mountain range.

Wade led the way. Then it was Abby, who was disguised as a young man. Then it was him and Lillian. And Jeremiah took up the rear. The trip would usually take a half hour, but because they had the heavy trunk, they had to go slower. Wade had been reluctant to bring the trunk with them, but Lillian would have to wear something, so she needed the clothes in it.

Abby had said Lillian was coming from the East, and Mic had heard those people could be outlandishly wealthy. Maybe that was why Charles had picked her. Just by looking at Lillian's clothes, Mic could tell she came from money. Something like that would definitely appeal to Charles. Now that he thought about it, her clothes were a dead giveaway that she was the one who was Charles' mail-order bride. The other woman's dress was much too simple. It was too drab and too old. Lillian's was undeniably new, and by the look of it, she spent more than a couple of dollars on it.

Well, that was no matter now. She wouldn't be marrying Charles at this point. She'd be marrying him. He wasn't sure she was going to like it, but he had to make sure if Charles did catch up to them, he couldn't marry her. If she had any idea what kind of man Charles was, she would be glad he and the others took her from the stagecoach. The problem, of course, was that she didn't know what Charles was like, and because of that, she might not believe him when he explained everything to her.

When they finally reached the abandoned cabin, the group let out a collective sigh of relief and brought their horses to a stop. He got down first, and then he held his arms out to help Lillian down.

She hesitated and glanced at the cabin that was beginning to show signs of neglect. No doubt, this was the last thing she had expected when she left her home back East. No. That wasn't quite right. The last thing she had expected was to be stolen from the stagecoach. The second to last thing she had expected was to be taken to a run-down cabin with a group of outlaws.

"We won't be here for long," he assured her. "We're going to get something to eat and hitch up your trunk to a travois. Then we'll be on our way again."

He opted not to tell her he was going to marry her. There was no need to have her running off while the horse was close by. He held his hand out to help her down. For a moment, he wasn't sure if she was going to accept it, but she took a deep breath and accepted his hand.

Abby removed her bandana and hat, revealing her dark red hair that was pulled up into a ponytail. "Hi there," she told Lillian. "I thought you might feel better if you knew you weren't the only girl in the group."

Lillian glanced around at the others, and Mic hurried to pull off his bandana so she could see his face. Jeremiah followed suit. Wade, however, hesitated.

"Come on, Wade," Mic called out. "Take the bandana off."

Rolling his eyes, Wade finally obeyed.

"I'm Abby," his sister told Lillian. "This here is my brother Mic. That one is my brother Wade. And the giant over there is Jeremiah. He's not related to us. He's just a childhood friend."

"I'm not a giant," Jeremiah argued.

"You're six-foot-five," Wade said. "Compared to everyone, you're a giant."

"Watch out, pipsqueak," Jeremiah said. "I'm likely to pound you into the ground for that kind of talk." Then Jeremiah gave Wade a playful punch, resulting in Wade grunting as he rubbed his arm.

With a chuckle, Abby turned her attention back to Lillian. "We're not a bad bunch of people. We don't go around abducting people from stagecoaches, but when we heard that Charles was getting a mail-order bride, we had to rescue you."

"Rescue me?" Lillian asked, her tone indicating that she didn't believe Abby.

"How much do you know about Charles Gray?" Abby asked.

Lillian hesitated but then said, "As much as any mail-order bride knows about her intended, I suppose. He said he owns a five-hundred-acre ranch and has a group of men under his employment."

Wade marched over to her. "Did he say anything about having a kid?"

Lillian backed up from him and bumped into Mic. She hurried to apologize and, probably deciding that Mic made a good barrier between her and Wade, she slipped behind Mic. "Yes," she told Wade. "He said he was a lonely widower who needed a mother for his child."

Wade's face grew bright red, and Mic held his hand up to stop him before he went around him to get to Lillian. "All she knows is what Charles told her. She doesn't know what kind of man he is. If you take a good look at her, you can see that."

Gritting his teeth, Wade studied her.

Mic couldn't help but feel sorry for her. She looked like a scared rabbit exposed to a pack of wolves. Her arms were wrapped around herself in a protective gesture, and her skin was as white as a ghost. Though Mic worried it might scare her even more, he put his arm around her shoulders in an attempt to comfort her.

"Charles has Wade's son," Mic softly told her. "That's why he's upset."

Lillian looked at Wade. "Charles didn't say anything about having your son. He said the boy is his. I can show you his missive if you want to see it."

"That's not necessary," Mic replied.

"Speak for yourself," Wade said. "I want to see it." He turned his gaze back to her. "Where is it?"

Lillian dug her hand into the pocket of her dress. "It's right here."

Mic winced at the way her voice trembled. He shot Wade a pointed look, hoping Wade would go easier on her.

But Wade ignored him.

When she gave the missive to him, he hurried to unfold it. He walked a few steps away from the group and read it. Then he uttered several curse words that made Mic's face warm in embarrassment. Maybe Abby was used to such talk, but he doubted Lillian was.

Wade returned to them. "Is this all you got?" he asked Lillian, his voice, thankfully, kinder than it had been before.

Lillian swallowed. "Yes. I answered his ad and sent him a missive. That was his response." She glanced at the others. "All his ad said was that he was looking for a young lady who'd never been married and could help him raise his child."

"We believe you," Mic assured her. He turned his gaze to Wade. "We believe her, don't we?"

"Yes," Wade snapped. "Yes, I do. He doesn't even refer to Lloyd by name." Wade threw the paper to the ground. Tears filled his eyes, and he quickly stormed away from the group.

"Lloyd is his two-year-old son," Abby told Lillian.

"I'm sorry," Lillian said. "I had no idea."

"You have nothing to be sorry for," Mic replied. "You did nothing wrong."

"You didn't," Abby hurried to add. "You'll have to forgive Wade. In our family, I might have gotten the red hair, but he got the temper."

"He has a good reason to be upset," Mic said. "Charles came in and stole Wade's land, killed his wife, and kept his son."

"He did all of that?" Lillian asked, eyes wide.

Mic nodded. "All in one night." Noting that Wade had gone off to a lone spot to sit, he added, "We couldn't let you go to someone like that. I might not have been born and raised back East where you come from, but out here, he who has the most guns and men makes the law around here. It's not a very civil territory."

Lillian's shoulders slumped, and he sensed her disappointment. This wasn't something she had expected when she'd agreed to come out here. But how could she have known what she was getting herself into? It was obvious by her fancy dress and trunk that she'd been used to a comfortable lifestyle. She'd probably had a nice home. Maybe a servant or two. Not a hint of sunlight had ever touched her face. So she'd been used to being inside, wearing a large hat, or carrying one of those fancy parasols that Abby considered to be a waste of money.

If he had to guess, Lillian hadn't cooked or cleaned a day in her life. Well, she was in for a shock when she saw his place. Her life wasn't going to be anything like what she was used to. Perhaps with Charles, she would have had some semblance of it. Charles did have a few servants. He could afford it with the money he'd stolen. But he would have been cruel to her, just as he'd been cruel to Wade's wife. Pushing away the unpleasant memory, he focused on the matter at hand.

"I bet you're hungry," Mic said. "When was the last time you ate?"

After a moment, she answered, "This morning. Just after dawn."

"You poor thing," Abby said, scanning her up and down. "You're thin enough as it is. We need to get you something to eat so you don't wither away. You have another day's journey ahead of you before you and Mic make it home."

Mic noted the way Lillian's eyes grew wide. He cleared his throat and gave Abby a quick shake of his head so she wouldn't say anymore. Not yet. It was too soon to be springing all of this on the poor woman. She'd just been abducted from the stagecoach and told her intended wasn't the man she'd expected. She didn't need to have everything else dumped on her. At least not right now.

"We all need to get something to eat," Mic spoke up after the awkward moment had passed. "Come." He encouraged Lillian to go into the cabin. "There's a table and some chairs in there. You make yourself as comfortable as you can. Abby, why don't you keep her company? I'm sure she'd like to have another woman around."

"Alright." With a smile, Abby slipped her arm around Lillian's and led her to the cabin.

Mic went to the leather sack attached to his steed and pulled out some pemmican. It wasn't much, but it would fill them up until nightfall. He glanced at the sky. If he had to guess, it was just past one in the afternoon. They still had a long way to go before the day was over. He didn't want Charles or his men finding them. Sure, this particular cabin was out of the way, and it was unlikely Charles or his men would find it, but it was still close enough to the stagecoach trail that they might.

Since Jeremiah was close by, he went over to him and gave him some pemmican.

"Are you sure you want to go through with this?" Jeremiah asked before he took a big bite of the food.

"Why not? She's pretty," Mic replied, feeling a bit foolish for voicing something a schoolboy might say.

"Sure, she is, but that doesn't mean she'll make a good wife."

"I can't take her to my house without doing the right thing."

Jeremiah swallowed his bite of pemmican then shot him a pointed look. "You don't have to take her to your bed."

"I didn't say I was planning on taking her to my bed." Not right away. She would need time to get used to him first.

"Then why get married?"

"Because… Because…" Unable to come up with a response, he shrugged.

Jeremiah's lips curled up into a knowing smile. "You want someone to warm your bed. That's why you wanted to get her from the stagecoach and marry her."

"No. I wanted to make sure she didn't end up with Charles. My ma wouldn't approve of me taking her to my home unless I married her first."

"I love the way you reason things out."

Mic sighed.

"I don't care if that's why you want to marry her," Jeremiah said. "I'm just glad you're not asking me to do it. I don't need a woman nagging at me for the rest of my life. I live alone, and it suits me just fine."

"Then we'll say I'm marrying her so you don't have to. We both know Wade's in no condition to marry anyone, so it's either you or me. I'm doing you a favor."

He chuckled and took another bite of pemmican. "Sure. We'll go with that." He glanced at the cabin. "When are you going to bring the eager bride out?"

"She needs to eat first."

"You're right. Give her one last meal before you give her the awful news."

Hiding his grin, Mic went over to Wade, who was wiping his eyes with his bandana. "I know this whole thing has been difficult for you. I promise you that we will get Lloyd, and after we get your son out of harm's way, we'll get the land back."

"Charles didn't just take our land and my son. He raped and killed my wife. I'm never getting her back, and the worst part is, I couldn't stop him from hurting her before he slit her throat."

"I know." After a moment, Mic offered him some pemmican. "You need to keep your strength up. For Lloyd's sake."

Wade took it and ate a small bite. "Are you really going to marry that woman in there?" He nodded toward the cabin.

"She's going to need somewhere to live, and it's best if we're married when I take her home."

Wade shook his head. "I'll never understand your sense of honor. Ever since we were kids, you were determined to do the right thing, no matter what."

"Well, Jeremiah would rather die than take a wife."

Wade shook his head. "If you want to marry Charles' mail-order bride, go ahead. I'm not going to stop you. Who knows? Maybe she'll make you happy."

Mic noted the bitterness in Wade's tone. Mic couldn't blame him. Wade had lost so much in the past year. If anyone deserved to be bitter, it was him. But Mic could tell his brother was struggling to keep his emotions under control, something that had to be difficult when everything had been taken from him.

"We're in this together," Mic finally said. "You're not alone. Jeremiah, Abby, and I will be with you when the time is right to get Lloyd and your land back."

Wade turned away from him, and Mic thought Wade was wiping his eyes again. Wade was a proud man. A tough man. He was older than both Mic and Abby, and he was used to being in control. Mic didn't blame Wade for not wanting to appear weak, but he was only human.

Knowing there was nothing else he could say to ease Wade's discomfort, Mic left him and headed for the cabin.

Chapter Three

"Once you hold a rattlesnake in your hand, there isn't anything that can scare you," Abby told Lillian. "You'll learn a lot out here about taking care of yourself. This wilderness will toughen you up fast. And don't think that just because you're a woman that you can't do it. Why, I wear pants and shoot a gun just like a man. Been doing that ever since I was little, too. I got to tell you, that fancy dress you got on has no place out here. Maybe you can cut it up and make curtains or a tablecloth out of it."

Lillian had taken her hat off, set it on the table, and put her face in her hands, but Abby didn't seem to realize that listening to her was giving her a headache. Well, that wasn't fair. Abby wasn't responsible for it. Having to leave the safety of the stagecoach and go on horseback to this cabin had been the beginning of the headache. Listening to Abby ramble on like they were having a tea party only made Lillian much more aware of the pain.

And she didn't dare ask Abby to quit. What if Abby got upset with her and shot her? What if she dumped a rattlesnake right on her lap? What if she ordered her brothers to leave so that Lillian was stuck here all by herself?

Lillian honestly didn't know if it'd be better to stay with this group or to be left alone. On one hand, there was no telling what a group of outlaws would do to her. But then, she didn't know the first thing about fending for herself.

Abby stopped rambling.

Surprised, Lillian looked up from her hands in time to see Mic coming into the cabin. He held out a piece of tough meat to Abby, who took it, and then turned to Lillian with a second piece.

"It's pemmican," he told Lillian. "I know it doesn't look like much, but it'll keep you full until we camp for the night."

"It's tough, but it's good," Abby assured her before taking a bite out of her ration.

After a moment, Lillian accepted it and then took a tentative bite. She slowly chewed it. Yes, it was definitely tough. She couldn't quite place the taste of it, though. It was heavy in fat. That was for sure. It was primarily made of meat. But she thought she detected some berries in it.

"It has a little honey to help with the taste," Mic told her. "I can make things that taste better than that. This is just to get us through the journey. Pemmican is good for keeping you full for a long time."

"It's a recipe he got from our ma," Abby added. "She came from the Lakota tribe. She was a gift to our pa for his help when some men tried to kill the people in her tribe."

"There are a lot of soldiers at Fort Laramie," Mic said as he sat down at the table. "That's north of us. Be glad you won't be there. It's not pleasant. There's a lot of tension between the Indians and the United States troops. We're heading further south, so we won't be affected by the fighting that might break out."

"Might?" Abby shot him a pointed look. "It'll definitely break out at some point. Be glad you're not going to live in Laramie with Charles."

"There's something else you should know about Charles." Mic took off his hat and ran his fingers through his dark hair, which had gotten sweaty from having worn the hat for so long. "He's our half-brother. We have the same father. Charles' mother died before our father married our mother. Wade,

Abby, and I are full-blooded siblings. There's been a lot of tension between Charles and us because of that."

He gestured to Abby and continued, "Our mother was from the Lakota tribe, and Charles never could accept her because of that. The ranch Charles is on belongs to Wade because our father left it to him in the will. I don't want to go into detail, but let's just say that our father didn't like the choices Charles had made." He paused, as if to consider how to continue, then added, "A year ago, Charles and his men stole the land from Wade and killed Wade's wife. He's currently holding Wade's son, Lloyd, as hostage. He says he'll kill Lloyd if we try to get the land back." He paused again. "Out here, when someone wants something and they have enough men fighting with him, he can take whatever he wants."

His voice drifted off then, and Lillian glanced at Abby. Abby's cheerful expression had turn into a solemn one. Given their reactions, whatever else Charles had done was probably worse than what she'd just learned. She shivered.

Under ordinary circumstances, she would think the two were only making this stuff up in order to make her sympathetic to them, but the fact that they had gone through all the trouble of taking her from the stagecoach without hurting anyone made her suspect they were telling her the truth.

Plus, she didn't get the feeling that they were lying. She'd had that feeling the moment her brother introduced her to Robert back in Virginia. Something in her had warned her that Robert wasn't the kind of person she could trust. And she'd been right. She couldn't trust him. She was getting no such vibe from Mic or Abby.

So where did that leave her? If Charles was as bad as, or worse, than Robert, then what was she supposed to do? Sure, she had money, but out here in the wilderness with nothing but mountains in view, she couldn't exactly take her trunk to town and start a new life.

Charles was in Laramie, and she didn't want to go there. She had no idea if there was another town nearby. She had no map, nor did she have a horse. She glanced around the cabin. Was she supposed to stay here? Was that why they'd brought her here?

"I know this is a lot to take in," Mic said, interrupting her thoughts. "I also realize it's not the kind of thing you wanted to hear since you came all the way into this rugged territory to marry Charles." Mic stopped and looked at Abby, who was taking another bite of the pemmican.

Abby glanced his way, and her eyes grew wide. "What?" she asked.

"I didn't realize this would be so awkward with you here," he told her.

Lillian frowned. What was awkward? Certainly, telling her about Charles couldn't be the thing he was referring to. Since they shared the same background, Abby was already aware of everything he'd been telling Lillian.

Abby's gaze went from him to Lillian. Then she took another bite of the pemmican and asked, "You want me to propose to her for you?"

Mic's face went bright red, and it took Lillian a moment to realize what Abby meant. Propose? As in marriage? But she didn't even know him. How did she know she could trust him? But she had planned to marry Charles, sight unseen, and Charles had turned out to be an unsavory character.

Mic shook his head in irritation but turned his attention to Lillian. "This wasn't exactly the way I had planned to suggest you and I get married, but due to my sister's big mouth," he shot Abby a pointed look, "I suppose this is a good time to bring up the subject. I don't have a lot. I got a small cabin at the foot of the mountain over that way." He gestured to the southwest. "I know it's not the kind of life you're used to, but

I got everything I need. You would have a place to live and food on the table. I'll be good to you. I'm nothing like Charles."

"None of us are like Charles," Abby added. "Charles takes after his mother, and she didn't believe in doing anything for anyone unless she benefited from it. We, on the other hand, take after our mother. She was a full-blooded Lakotan, and her people believe that we should take care of others. Happiness comes from doing things for each other."

"The point," Mic interrupted, "is that since you're not marrying Charles, you'll need somewhere to stay." He paused and turned to his sister. "Can I have a moment alone with Lillian?"

Lillian shifted in her chair. Did she trust Mic enough to be alone with him? She studied him. He didn't seem to be anything like Robert. He hadn't talked down to her, nor had he talked down to his sister or brothers. He hadn't been rough with her in the way he'd touched her when he helped her out of the stagecoach and getting on or off the horse. And even though it was apparent Abby had said way more than he was comfortable with, Mic hadn't yelled at her.

Those were all good indicators that he was someone she could trust. She released her breath and relaxed as Abby left the cabin.

Mic turned toward Lillian. "I know this isn't what you expected when you came out to this territory, but the only way I can think of to protect you is by marrying you. I promise you that I'm not a bad person. I might have some faults, but they're minor."

"Oh?"

"I've been told by Abby and Wade that I can be too particular when it comes to how I garden. Every row has to be exactly straight, and each plant has to be spaced out evenly. I use a ruler when I put the seeds in. I'll even dig up seeds and plant them in again if I get to the end of the row and decide I don't like how far apart or how close they are. They say it makes me odd."

The image of him being that fussy about planting seeds made her chuckle.

The corners of his lips curled up. "They say a normal person would just eyeball how far apart everything should be. Maybe they're right, but this is the way I've been growing things in gardens since I was ten. I'm old enough now where I'm set in my ways."

"You don't look old. You look like you're twenty-two or twenty-three."

"I'm twenty-four. Wade is thirty-one. Abby's twenty-two. She's the youngest of all of us, but she knows how to take care of herself. She's been able to hold her own ever since she was fourteen." He paused then asked, "How old are you?"

"I'm twenty-three. Where I come from, that is old for a woman. I should have married sooner than that."

"What made you say no to all the proposals you were getting?"

"Who said I got proposals?"

"A pretty thing like you must have had some offers."

He would be wrong about that, but she was so pleased he had said she was pretty that she wasn't about to correct him. Growing up, her parents and brother often commented she should be the best at playing the piano, the best dressed, or the most well versed in literature so that she would have something to offer a suitor. The agreement her brother worked out with Robert wasn't the same thing as getting an offer. That had been strictly a financial arrangement.

"If you went into Laramie," Mic continued, "you'd have a line of men rushing to marry you. Ranchers, the soldiers at the fort, and Indians. I'm just glad I got to you before they did."

She shook her head, but he seemed to believe it. Perhaps it was because there was a shortage of women in the area. Any woman could come into this territory and be attractive. It was the only thing that made sense since he was being sincere.

"I can cook," Mic added. "I catch my own game, skin it, and cook it up. I can do better than pemmican, too."

"I think you mentioned something about that earlier," she replied, unable to stop herself from teasing him.

"Well, I thought it wouldn't hurt to remind you. Just in case you're thinking of heading for Laramie to get a better offer. I don't care how much some of those men earn. They will never cook a steak as good as I can. You ought to keep that in mind, especially since you have to eat every day."

She laughed at his joke.

"I'm not saying that you have to eat steak every day," he added, his eyes twinkling as he leaned toward her. "I don't mind it myself, but it's hard to catch game all the time. I shouldn't misrepresent what our marriage would be like. I'm not only good at knowing what to do with meat, but I also make good use of the vegetables, fruits, and nuts on my property. If you want to eat well, you'll pick me to be your husband."

"What would I offer you if I was your wife? Would it be taking care of the home?"

"Sure, that would be some of the arrangement. But mostly, companionship. I don't get to see a lot of people. Jeremiah's a recluse. He lives in a hovel. Abby stays in town. Wade is in a hideout so Charles won't find him. As long as Wade's alive, Charles knows Wade might take the land back." For a moment, the laughter left his eyes. "It hasn't been an easy year for any of us, but Wade's been hit the hardest. Maybe someday I'll go more into all of that. We don't have much time to stay in this spot. I asked Jeremiah to come along because he's a friend of the family and a preacher."

"He is?" She wouldn't have expected someone who looked more like a grizzly bear than a man to be a man of God.

Jeremiah had a long dark beard and wore clothes that had seen better days.

"He's no longer presiding over a church, but he still has the qualifications to go back to one if he wants to. Anyway, I asked him to come along so he could marry us. I wouldn't feel right taking you out to my place without doing things the right way. It may not be as civilized out in these parts as it is back East, but I want to do everything properly. Our mother wouldn't have wanted me to do it any other way."

Lillian thought it was sweet that even if his mother wasn't alive, he wanted to please her. And he did have a nice sense of humor. She couldn't recall the last time she'd laughed.

She took a deep breath. She'd been ready to marry a complete stranger today. She hadn't even met Charles. A letter didn't reveal everything a person needed to know to make a good decision about marrying someone. She'd been ready to do it on blind faith. At least she had met and talked to Mic. Already, she knew him more than she knew Charles, and he seemed like a nice person. Also, she felt comfortable with the idea of marrying him, and she hadn't felt that with Robert.

She released her breath and nodded. "Alright. I'll marry you."

Chapter Four

As everyone assembled for the wedding, Mic still couldn't believe it. Lillian had said yes. He had hoped she'd say yes. He wouldn't have asked her if he didn't want to marry her, but he was sure that she wouldn't feel safe in marrying someone who had taken her from a stagecoach. He wouldn't have blamed her if she said no.

But he was awfully glad she'd said yes. Jeremiah was such a recluse that it was hard to tell when he'd make the trip out to see Mic, and he was the only person outside of Laramie that could perform a wedding ceremony. Mic didn't dare go into Laramie until Charles was no longer a threat. It was because of Charles that he and Wade were considered outlaws. Charles had friends in influential places, and it hadn't taken much to pin the bank robbery on them.

Since Abby was a woman, Charles didn't worry about her. By the time she was learning how to use a knife and gun to protect herself, he had already been on his own. And this gave Mic and Wade an advantage. She lived in town as a teacher, and she was instrumental in figuring out what Charles was up to.

If Lillian went to Laramie, she'd see the Wanted posters for Mic and Wade all over the place. It didn't matter that Mic and Wade hadn't robbed the bank. The fact that they were accused of the crime would have been enough to make her go running to another man.

At some point, he would have to tell her everything. He wasn't sure how he was going to do that. He didn't even know when he should tell her about it. She was a prim and proper lady. She'd been brought up in a genteel society. The idea of marrying an outlaw—even though he was really innocent—might be too much for her to deal with. It was better that she get to know him first. That way she would understand he wasn't the person the posters made him out to be. He only hoped that when the time came for him to tell her that she would understand why he didn't do it sooner.

"Alright, now that we got everyone to agree to partake in this wedding," Jeremiah said as he wiped the dust off the cover of the Book of Common Prayer. He opened it and turned to the table of contents. "It's been so long since I used this that I don't even remember where the wedding vows are. Now, if we were doing a funeral, I would go directly to page thirty-two."

Abby grimaced. "That's morbid, Jeremiah."

Jeremiah turned the pages. "Why? People around here die more than they marry."

Noting the worried expression on Lillian's face, Mic took her hand. He wasn't sure she would welcome the touch. Not so soon. Not so shortly after they met. And especially not since she'd only agreed to marry him five minutes ago. But he had hoped to set her mind at ease since Abby was right; no one wanted to think of death right before a wedding. Thankfully, Lillian didn't pull her hand out of his. At least she was willing to let him offer her some comfort, even if it was a small one.

"Well, no one is dying today," Mic told Jeremiah. "This is a happy occasion. It's the beginning of something new. So you don't need to look so glum."

Jeremiah looked up from the book. "I left the preacher's life behind me. I don't exactly enjoy going back to it, even if it is for a few minutes."

Well, this comment wasn't any more encouraging than talk of death, but since Jeremiah started reading from the book, Mic kept his mouth shut.

Mic glanced at Lillian, hoping she wasn't upset by Jeremiah's lack of enthusiasm. She didn't seem to be. When she glanced his way, he offered her a smile, and she offered him one in return. Breathing a sigh of relief, he turned his attention back to Jeremiah. Good. She was going to go through with this marriage after all.

"Marriage is, above and all things, honorable." Jeremiah paused and then shot Mic and Lillian a pointed look. "That means if you're going to do this, then you need to take it seriously. Too many people think the vows don't mean anything, but they do. Marriage is important. It's the merging of two lives together. You have to be willing to go through the good and bad. It's not always going to be easy and fun. There are going to be some rough times. And out here in this wild territory, there's a tendency to forget that the rough times often outweigh the good. So be sure you're not going to give up on each other just because things get tough."

Mic hesitated for a moment before saying, "I'm pretty sure all of that isn't in your book."

"It is," Jeremiah replied. "It's not so much in words, but it's there. It says all of the better or for worse, in sickness and in health, and richer or poor phrases. I could go into all of that, or I could remind you two that things aren't always going to be wonderful. As long as you will stay together no matter what happens, then I can join you as husband and wife. Otherwise, I'm not going to do it."

"Of course, we're going to stay together no matter what," Mic said. "You've known me since we were children. We might not be brothers, but we very well could be with the way you were over at my house all the time. Sometimes Ma would count you as one of her own."

Jeremiah glanced over at Wade who refused to meet his gaze. Turning his gaze back to Mic, he said, "You still got to promise it. If not to me, then to Lillian and God."

"I promise. No matter what, I'm going to stay by Lillian's side." He looked at Lillian and squeezed her hand. "Forever."

She smiled at him. "I promise to do that, too." Then, as if remembering Jeremiah, she looked to him. "Forever."

"Alright," Jeremiah said, seeming to be satisfied. "You are now husband and wife. You can kiss the bride if you want."

Mic did want to kiss her, but with Jeremiah, Wade, and Abby staring at him, he hesitated. "I'm not so sure I want an audience," he told them.

"Oh, come on. Give her a kiss," Abby said, nudging him in the shoulder. "It won't hurt."

"I know it won't hurt," Mic replied. "I just don't want everyone gawking at us like they've never seen anyone kiss before."

Abby gasped and put her hand to her chest. "What do you take us for? We used to watch our parents kiss all the time. It was sweet that they loved each other. You ought to kiss your wife to let her know you're going to love her, too."

There was more to love than a simple kiss, but since Abby wasn't going to stop pestering him about it until he did it, Mic turned to Lillian and gave her a quick kiss. Even the brief contact made his lips tingle.

"Is that all?" Abby asked.

Why was she still bugging him about this? Mic groaned. "I kissed her."

"I meant you should give her a deep, passionate kiss. Let her know how happy you are to be with her."

"The kiss he did was fine," Wade interrupted.

Mic silently thanked him for stepping into the conversation. When Abby got started, she could keep going.

"We should head out," Wade added. "It won't be long before Charles realizes Lillian's not coming. He'll start looking for us."

"He's right," Jeremiah agreed as he shut the book. "We've spent too much time here as it is. I know an unmarked trail that will take us to the river. From there, we all go our separate ways."

"That won't happen until tomorrow," Mic told Lillian, just so she knew they'd be spending the rest of this day with his family.

Lillian offered a nod but didn't say anything. He couldn't blame her. This was all new to her. Not only was she adjusting to a new area and a new lifestyle, she was adjusting to new people, too. And who knew what she thought of the lot of them? Abby was overly cheerful about everything. Jeremiah had a tendency to act like the best part of his life was over, even though he was only thirty-four. Wade had a lot of personal grief to deal with and a son to get back.

As for him... Well, Mic was tired of being alone all the time. He wanted someone to live with him, and who better than a woman he was married to? Even now, he felt less alone in the world by holding Lillian's hand.

"Alright," Wade spoke up, "let's get onto that unmarked trail."

From there, the group got ready to head out, and that meant Mic had to stop touching Lillian. It was a shame, too. He was enjoying it. But then, he would get to ride on the horse with her, and now that they were married, he didn't have to feel guilty for thinking of how nice it was when her body was pressed right up against his. He hadn't expected that when he and his family planned for her to ride with him on his horse. It had just made the most sense since he was hoping to marry her.

But all the way from the stagecoach to this cabin, he'd been thrilled to be so close to her. Fortunately, no one seemed to notice. And now if anyone did, he would just remind them she was his wife. He was supposed to find pleasure in riding a horse with her.

Mic got his horse and helped her onto the saddle. This time when he got up behind her, he didn't fight the thrill he experienced. Instead, he put his arm around her waist and drew her closer to him.

He heard someone let out a chuckle and turned his gaze over to Abby. Abby mouthed, *You're grinning like an idiot.*

Mic immediately curbed his enthusiasm. While it was fine to show his enthusiasm for sitting with Lillian, he didn't need to make it so obvious that even Abby noticed. His virginal sister should be the easiest one in the group to fool. If she caught on, then he was overdoing it.

He glanced over at Lillian to see if she had noticed the exchange between him and Abby, but she was looking forward. He was going to assume she hadn't. It was better that way.

He cleared his throat. "Is everyone ready?"

"Yep," Jeremiah said. "Though not as ready as you are." He shot him a knowing look and wiggled his eyebrows.

Mic glanced at Wade who smirked at him in a way that let him know he knew exactly what Mic was ready for.

Recalling that he had every right to be excited about being with his wife, Mic told Jeremiah, "*My wife* and I will be happy to follow you to the unmarked trail up ahead."

Jeremiah snorted but didn't say anything as he urged his horse forward.

"I think it's nice that you're happy to be with Lillian," Abby said, not realizing, of course, that his thoughts were more sexual than they were emotional. "It's a sign that things will be good between you."

Smiling, Abby snapped the reins of her horse and followed after Wade and Jeremiah.

Since Mic wasn't sure what to say to Lillian, he settled for giving her waist a light squeeze then urged his horse forward, content to enjoy the feel of her pressed up nicely to him.

***

The day was such a blur that Lillian had trouble keeping up with everything that was happening. When she had envisioned her life out in this territory, she never once imagined being taken from the stagecoach, marrying someone other than Charles, and then taking a horseback ride across rugged terrain. Soon they would be going up a mountain. For the moment, they were still on pretty level ground. Thanks to her childhood experience of riding a horse, she wasn't nearly as frightened as she probably would have been otherwise. There was something calming about riding the horse. It was familiar to her. It gave her some sense of normalcy in a new place with people she'd never met until today.

The most notable person she'd met, of course, was the man she'd just married. He seemed like a good man. He had a nice sense of humor, and he was gentle with her. Having his arm around her waist wasn't the least bit uncomfortable. Up to today, she hadn't done more than dance with a man at a ball. She'd never been as close to one as she was with Mic. She was pressed right up against him, and though he didn't look it from his clothes, she could feel the muscles in his chest and arms.

She'd heard that men out West often had to work with their hands. They did much more physical labor then men she was used to. She now had no doubt the rumors were true. Her brother was a scrawny fellow. When he hugged her after their parents died, she could feel there wasn't much to him. She often thought he only hugged her because he was expected to offer her some comfort in front of the others at the funeral. She hadn't fooled herself into thinking her brother had done it because he cared about her. It was all for show. To make people think he was a good older brother.

She didn't want to think of her brother. In fact, she didn't want to think about her life back in Virginia. All she wanted to do was put her past life behind her and move on to a better future. It was why she answered a mail-order bride ad. Otherwise, she would have ended up with Robert, and he was much worse than her brother.

The horse dipped down into a ravine, and she grabbed the saddle horn in surprise.

Mic's arm tightened around her waist. "Don't worry. I won't let you fall."

Her face warmed, more from his touch than from thinking she might fall off the horse. They went back up the ravine, and, once more, she relaxed against him.

"The terrain can get rough through here," Mic said. "It's a good route if you want your privacy. Very few come this way."

That was good. It meant she could hide better from Robert. He would never think to come all the way out here to find her.

"There are three more ravines coming up ahead. I'll give you a warning when they come up."

If she had been paying attention to the path in front of them, she would have seen it. With everything being so fresh in her mind over her hasty departure from Virginia, it was natural that she wasn't concerned about the path they were traveling.

But now, she took a moment to study her surroundings. They were heading for a group of trees that lined the base of a mountain. From the looks of it, they were going to pass through the trees and then head toward a clearing that would take them to another mountain.

In front of her and Mic, Jeremiah, Wade, and Abby rode in silence. There was a good distance between each of them. No one would overhear if she and Mic talked.

After a moment of debating whether or not to ask the question, Lillian ventured, "Can I ask you why Jeremiah stopped being a preacher, or is that too personal to discuss?"

"You can ask me anything. You're my wife," Mic replied.

His breath tickled her ear as he spoke. She smiled but resisted the urge to wiggle against him.

"Jeremiah and his wife lost their baby," Mic continued. "Soon after that, his wife divorced him, and he's been living by himself in the mountainside ever since."

"That's terrible."

"I know. He hasn't been the same since. The whole experience changed him. Believe it or not, he used to be as cheerful as Abby."

He was right. It was hard for her to believe Jeremiah used to be as cheerful as Abby. In fact, it was hard for her to believe anyone could be as cheerful as Abby.

"That's a shame Jeremiah and his wife lost their baby," she said. "It makes no sense to me why babies die."

"It makes no sense to me, either, but it's a good reminder to appreciate each day that we have."

She supposed he was right. There were two things a person could not pick. One was the day they were born; the second was the day they died. All they could do was make choices that would benefit them.

Without a doubt, she knew she had made the right choice in leaving Virginia. If she hadn't, her life would've been meaningless. It would've been filled with going from one ball to another...hosting one dinner party after another... She would've been stuck doing mindless things. Things that wouldn't have mattered with people who didn't care about her...and people she didn't care about.

Coming to the Wyoming Territory had been more than escaping a marriage to Robert. It had been about saving herself. She still wasn't quite sure how she was saving herself. She could only hope the chance—the risk—she'd taken would pay off.

The horse stepped into another ravine, and once again, Mic's arm tightened around her waist.

Deep in her gut, she felt that she had made the right decision in marrying him, though there was no proof to back that up. She felt safe with him. Safer than she had in a very long time. This particular day wasn't going the way she'd planned, but she had made the choice to spend the rest of her life with Mic. It was one of the things she'd had control over, and she suspected she would be glad she'd took this leap of faith in the years to come.

Chapter Five

That evening, the group stopped to camp for the night. Since they were far from any homesteads on the outskirts of town, Mic, Wade, Jeremiah, and Abby felt it was safe to make a campfire. The day had been a long one. Mic was exhausted. He could tell the others were exhausted, too. Lillian was probably more exhausted than all of them combined. For one, she had started her day in a stagecoach, and two, she wasn't used to traveling on horseback through rough terrain like they were.

Mic could only guess what she was thinking. The day had not gone at all the way she had planned. She was supposed to be with Charles tonight. By now, she would have married him, and at this moment, they would probably be in bed, consummating their marriage.

But instead, she was with him, and there would be no chance of consummating the marriage tonight. Nor would there be a bed to sleep in. They would have to lie on the ground in the open field, vulnerable to the whims of nature. Before they did that, however, they had to eat dinner.

"I know you're not used to having what we're going to eat," he told her, "but when you're out here—in the middle of nowhere—you pretty much take whatever you can get."

As if to demonstrate what he was saying was true, Wade shot a bird from the sky. It landed several feet from them. Abby shot a rabbit, and Jeremiah was gathering some grasshoppers.

"I can't promise any of those critters will taste any good, but if you eat enough of them, you'll be full for the night," Mic continued, hoping the reminder that she didn't have to go to sleep hungry would motivate her to eat the food they were bringing to the camp.

Though her face paled, she didn't protest.

Good. As soon as she got used to living this kind of life, the easier things would be for her.

"I promise that once we get to my home, you won't have to eat grasshoppers, though when it comes to meat, you take pretty much whatever you can get. I promise that the animals I catch will taste better than they look."

Before Lillian could ask him what kinds of animals he ate, Abby came over to them. "My favorite is snake. The best thing about snakes is that you not only get to eat the meat, but you can also make boots and belts out of their skin."

Noting the way Lillian's face paled even more, Mic told his sister, "Maybe we shouldn't talk about this kind of stuff right now. I want Lillian to have as much of an appetite as possible so she doesn't go hungry for the night."

Abby nodded. "You're right. Just wait until she sees what happens when you skin animals. I have a feeling she'll be fainting when she sees all that blood. That is, if she makes it that far. I remember the first time Pa showed us how to do it, and I couldn't believe it when he had us remove the bladder and the intestines first." She glanced over at Lillian. "You don't want to contaminate your food with urine and feces."

Mic thought he saw Lillian wobble on her feet. If Abby kept talking, there was really a good chance Lillian might pass out. Mic hurried to put his arm around Lillian so she didn't fall over.

Lillian managed to steady herself. "I'm afraid it's going to take me a while to adjust to all of this," she said in barely a whisper.

"Don't worry," Mic assured her. "I don't expect you to be up for all of this right away. I know it's going to take time. I just ask that you be patient as you adjust to your new life."

"I was just about to ask you to be patient with me. I feel so inept."

"I never lived back East, but I know that life here is a lot different from how it is there. I just hope you won't regret coming out here."

"Enough talking," Abby interrupted. "We need to eat so we can get to sleep. The sooner we get to sleep, the sooner we can head out in the morning."

Abby was right. Though they had made good progress during the day, there was still a long way to go. He would like to make it home by tomorrow night, if possible.

"Are you ready to eat?" Jeremiah called out.

"As ready as we'll ever be," Mic replied, answering for both him and Lillian.

He didn't think he could do anything else to prepare Lillian for the meal that was about to be set before her. He gave Lillian's waist a light squeeze. "Try not to think about what you're eating while you're eating it. It'll help things go down easier."

She nodded, and the three went over to the campfire to help Jeremiah and Wade with the food they had retrieved for the evening.

***

That night as Mic slept, he was having a good dream. A very good dream. In it, he and Lillian were making love beneath the stars. He could feel every curve of her body, hear every sigh she made, and feel every move she made against him. It was the most wonderful dream he'd ever had.

And then he woke up to the morning light.

At once, the dream shattered around him. But even as he became aware of the ground beneath him and the others who were still sleeping, he felt someone's hand right over his erection. Eyebrows furrowed, he looked over at the person he was holding, just to make sure it was Lillian and not someone else.

He breathed a sigh of relief. It was her.

Yes, he remembered lying down with her on the ground and wrapping them both in his blanket. He had been so exhausted that he fell asleep right away. He imagined she had done the same, though, for all he knew, it might've taken her longer to fall asleep simply because this was all new to her.

"You'd do well to remember we have a long day ahead of us," Wade called out.

Mic looked over at his brother who was sorting through his camping gear.

"If you wanted me to get up, why didn't you just say so?" he asked.

"I wasn't asking you to get up." Wade shot him a pointed look. "I just think you shouldn't be so obvious about how excited you are to be married."

Mic's face warmed. He glanced at the others, thankful they were still asleep. He wiggled away from Lillian and placed the blanket around her so she wouldn't get cold without him there to warm her up.

Mic went away from the group so he could relieve his bladder in private, or at least as much in private as the situation allowed. Then he returned to Wade, who gave him a knowing smirk.

Mic sat beside his brother and whispered, "Just because you were once a married man, it doesn't give you the right to give me such a hard time."

Wade shrugged. "Well, there are benefits to being married. I think Jeremiah's right, though. The only reason you wanted to marry her was to have a woman in your bed."

Mic pulled out the pot from Wade's leather sack and set it aside. "That's not the only reason I wanted to get married.

There's a lot more to it than that. It gets lonely out there at the cabin all by myself. Ever since Charles chased us off the ranch, I've had very little interaction with anybody."

"I'm going to get that ranch back if it's the last thing I do."

"We'll make sure it isn't the last thing you do. You have a son. He's already lost his mother. He doesn't need to lose his father, too."

"He's not going to lose me. When we go in, we're going to have a plan."

"This plan better involve a lot more men than what we currently have. Have you seen the number of people Charles has working for him?"

"I know very well how many are working for him. That's why we have to think about how we're going to do this. If we can sneak in, we can do it ourselves."

Mic watched as Wade poured water into the pot. "It's not going to be as easy as you think. Charles has men all through the place. You can't just sneak in there."

"Yes, we can. We grew up in that house. We know where everything is. That gives us an advantage."

Mic heard someone stirring nearby, and he saw Abby getting up.

"We're going to get my son," Wade said. "And we're not going to involve others. We can't afford to let someone tell Charles what we're up to."

Unfortunately, Wade made a good point. The less people who knew what they were going to do, the better. He just hoped when the time came to act, they were going to be successful.

***

The second day of riding with Mic on the horse was much easier than the first had been. Now that Lillian had gotten used to Mic holding her, she could relax. She still had much to learn about her new husband, but that would've been the case no matter who she had married yesterday. She did like him, though.

So when it came time for Abby, Wade, and Jeremiah to go their separate ways along the path, Lillian didn't feel a rush of panic overtake her. Instead, she found that she was looking forward to being alone with Mic. It'd be nice to get a chance to know him better.

Once they were alone on the winding narrow path leading up the side of the mountain, she asked, "How much longer will it be until we reach your home?"

Mic squeezed her waist gently with his arm. "I think you mean our home."

Catching the playful tone in his voice, she smiled. "You're right. *Our* home. When will we be there?"

"By nightfall. This terrain slows the horse down. If we were to walk, we would make better time, but then, we wouldn't be able to bring your trunk with us, and I want to make sure you have your clothes."

"I don't mind. The scenery is lovely." Just as Millie, her traveling companion on the stagecoach had said, the mountains were beautiful.

"I'm glad you like it," Mic replied. "I hope you don't miss your hometown too much."

"Virginia was pleasant, but long ago, I learned it's not where you're at that matters; it's who you're with."

"I can already say that I enjoy being with you."

Pleased, she admitted, "I like being with you, too." Back home, she never would've been this forward with a man. But out here in the Wild West, in this untamed territory, she didn't feel the restrictions that used to keep her from acting so boldly.

When they reached a creek, Mic pulled the reins so that the horse stopped.

"We'll take a break," he told Lillian. "The horse could use a rest, and I don't know about you, but I'm ready to eat."

Lillian wasn't so sure she wanted to eat, given what she'd had for dinner the night before. She'd had to force down the oatmeal Wade and Mic had made that morning. She only did that because she didn't want to be rude. But every time she thought about eating, all she could see were rabbits, birds, and grasshoppers being roasted in the campfire.

She did, however, welcome the opportunity to sit down and rest for a while. Though being on the horse did not require her to do any physical labor, it had still worn her out. It was probably because she wasn't used to riding one all day long. In the past, she'd only ridden horses for pleasure, and that was for no more than an hour at a time. Life out here was going to be a lot different from what she was used to, and the sooner she got used to it, the better. Regardless, she really didn't think she could eat anything right now. She only hoped that Mic would understand.

Mic got off the horse first and then extended his hand to help her down. Well, she had to admit that he was a gentleman. He might be stuck in rugged terrain and he might be wearing clothes none of the men would be caught dead in back in Virginia, but he was, at his core, a gentleman. It was almost enough to convince her to give another fried insect, bird, or rabbit a second try. Almost. But not enough. Not when her stomach roiled in protest. She was sure the last thing he wanted was a woman who might throw up in front of him.

Once she was down from the horse, she said, "Please don't take this the wrong way, but I don't have an appetite right now. Do you mind if I wait until later to eat?"

Still holding her hand, he gave it a reassuring squeeze. "I don't mind. I figured after last night, it was going to take you a while before you were able to eat anything again. Frankly, I was surprised you were able to eat at all this morning."

Relaxing, she chuckled. "I did have trouble eating. It was hard not to think about what I had last night."

"I don't expect you to adjust to this life right away. I know it's going to take time."

"Thank you. Not all men would be so understanding." Robert and her brother being two of them. But she didn't want to say that. This was a nice moment, and she didn't want to ruin it.

He paused for a moment, glancing at the ground before he looked back up to make eye contact with her, as if to gather the courage to say something. Finally, he spoke, "I know we just got married yesterday, and we really don't know each other that well. But I was wondering if I could kiss you."

Her heart gave an unexpected flutter. Despite the shyness welling up within her, she replied, "I'd like a kiss."

His smile growing wider, he lowered his head to hers and gave her a kiss. The action, though brief, sent a spark right through her. This was nice. It was something she could get used to. And it was nice to know that she would get to do this more in the future.

"I've been wanting to do that again ever since the first one," he said.

Surprised, she asked, "Why did you wait so long to kiss me a second time then?"

"Because I didn't want the others around when I finally did it. It was bad enough that Jeremiah and Wade kept giving me knowing looks."

"What kind of knowing looks?"

"Just looks. Looks men give other men when they know they really want to be alone with a woman. Especially one they're married to."

She wasn't sure why the topic should make him blush, but his face was bright red and he ended up looking away from her. This must be one of those things only men understood.

"At the risk of sounding bolder than I probably should, I like to kiss. And I wouldn't mind it if you kissed me again."

His gaze went back to hers, and seeming more confident than before, he wrapped her in his arms and brought her closer to him. Then he was kissing her again. This time his lips stayed there longer, giving her a better chance to enjoy the thrill of being so intimately entwined with him. She melted against him, thinking there just might be nothing better than sharing a moment like this with someone as wonderful as Mic.

When the kiss ended, he led the horse to the creek so the animal could get something to drink. Then he grabbed some jerky from his sack and sat with her near a group of trees so that they could both rest up before they continued their journey.

Chapter Six

By the time they arrived at his homestead, the sun was getting ready to set for the night. Lillian had to be exhausted. They had woken up around the time of dawn, and they spent the entire day riding on the horse. She just might be so tired that she would fall asleep as soon as she got into bed.

He was hoping this wouldn't be the case because all day long he'd been holding her and imagining what it would be like to finally be in bed with her. But if she was too tired, he would let her sleep. It was the least he could do after he had dragged her all the way out to the mountainside to live with him. He would just have to take care of his basic needs so that he would be able to get some sleep as well. God knew he wasn't able to get much sleep the night before.

As he led the horse past the cabin, he said, "This is it. Welcome home."

Such as it was. The cabin was really no more than a kitchen with a loft. Also, there wasn't too much to the barn. It was enough to house his cow and a horse. To the side of the barn was the henhouse. And behind the barn was a small pasture for the horse and cow when he let them out during the day. Further up the property, behind the cabin, was where he kept the garden. In the garden, he had rows of vegetables and some tomatoes that he was growing. Bushes of berries were nearby.

When they reached the barn, Mic got off the horse first and then he helped Lillian down. "What do you think? I know it's nothing like what you had back East, but I hope it'll do."

She smiled at him. "I think it's lovely."

"I should have probably waited until you were inside the cabin before I asked for your opinion. It's not as big as it looks from the outside."

She shrugged. "More space is no good if you have rooms that never get used."

Her comment surprised him. Just what kind of home had she come from? If she had rooms that went unused, then she must've been in a big one. He glanced over at her trunk, which the horse had been pulling on a travois. Had she been an heiress? No, probably not. An heiress would never marry someone as common as him, much less come all the way out here to live in this rugged territory. But she had come from money. That much was obvious. That trunk was made of good material, and she conducted herself with the kind of grace and charm he'd heard wealthy people possessed. Could she ever be happy out here with him? There was no way he could give her anything like the kind of life she'd had back East.

"Do you want me to help you bring in the trunk?" she asked.

"No, I can carry it. It would help if you opened the front door to the cabin, though," he replied as he went over to the trunk.

With a nod, she hurried over to the cabin and did as he wished. He picked up the trunk and carried it into his home...or rather, their home.

He almost wished he had taken her up on her offer to help him. The thing was heavier than he remembered, but when he had put it on the travois, Wade had helped him. So as not to seem weak, he set it on the floor in the small kitchen and said, "I'll take it up to the loft tomorrow."

"The loft?"

He gestured to the ladder that led up to the small room on the second floor. "That's where I sleep. There's a bed up there and a small dresser. You'll have to hunch down when you're up there, but there's enough room for the trunk."

She nodded and scanned the cabin. There was a cookstove that also operated as a fireplace in the winter time, a kitchen table, shelves along the wall to hold his cooking supplies, and two rocking chairs. The other chairs were outside. The only reason the place had a total of four chairs was because Jeremiah, Wade, and Abby would pay him a visit from time to time.

She turned her attention back to him and smiled. "I like it. It's cozy."

She was smiling, so cozy had to be good. He wasn't familiar with the term. He couldn't recall anything in this rugged territory being "cozy".

He gestured to her trunk. "I'll let you get ready for bed while I take care of the animals." And then, as an afterthought, he added, "Unless there's something else you need right now."

She shook her head. "I have everything I need, thank you. I think I'll get ready for bed and then go up to the loft."

He wondered if she meant that she would be waiting for him in bed or if she planned to go right to sleep. But he didn't dare ask, just in case he didn't like the answer. He would just go outside and take care of the animals. Then when he came back in here, he would know what her intentions were. Without another word, he left the cabin.

***

Lillian lit the kerosene lamp and opened her trunk. Good. All of her things were still there, untouched and in good condition. She sorted through her shirtwaists, skirts, extra pair of chemise and bloomers, two pairs of stylish boots, two hats, and handkerchiefs and drawstring purse. She sighed. They were much too fine for living out here, but they had been the most durable clothes she had when she was packing. She was going to be sorely out of place in this environment. Why didn't she think to ask Charles what kind of clothes she should bring?

She shook her head. Never mind the clothes. What she really needed to know was if the money was still in her trunk, or if someone who'd handled this trunk while she was on the train had discovered her secret.

The contents of her trunk were the only reason she risked leaving Virginia. Yes, she had taken a big risk, but the money belonged to her. She wasn't going to let Robert get his greedy hands on it. She had to take it with her. She'd do so again if she had the chance.

She took the clothes out so that the wooden bottom of her trunk was all she could see. Her fingers ran along the edge of the wood paneling until she felt the indentation carved into it. She pulled on it and the paneling came up with it.

She'd evenly distributed the gold and silver coins she'd placed in drawstring purses along the edge of the trunk. She removed a couple layers of petticoats and counted all of the bills in her possession, making sure they were all there.

Good. They were.

It hadn't been easy to access her inheritance, but she had, and Robert would never see a single penny of the $10,000.

She wrapped the bills in the petticoats and settled them between the drawstring purses. Then she returned the wood paneling to its proper place and made sure it was secure. She carefully returned all of the clothes except for her chemise to her trunk, mindful of the order she was using so she'd know if anyone tampered with this trunk.

Not that she could imagine who would find it this far in the mountainside. It was highly unlikely that Robert would find her all the way out here. Mic's home was further removed from civilization than Charles Gray's ranch was.

She bit her lower lip. She should probably tell Mic about the money. No. There was no *probably* about it. She *would* tell him.

She debated how to do so as she got undressed and then slipped on her chemise. There was a good reason the trunk was heavier than he had expected. Maybe that was a good place to start. Maybe she'd ask him if he wondered why her trunk was so heavy. And when he said he did wonder about it, she would explain why.

When she was done getting ready for bed, she checked the sky. By now the sun had set all the way, leaving the sky with a deep rich blue color. Had it not been for the kerosene lamp, there would be no light at all in the cabin. She looked out the kitchen window but didn't see anything.

The door opened, and she jumped. As soon as she realized it was Mic, she put her hand over her heart and laughed. "I didn't hear you approaching the cabin."

"I'm sorry. I didn't mean to scare you." He stopped talking as soon as his gaze went to her chemise.

Her body went warm while he scanned her. The chemise was such a thin piece of fabric. At the moment, she felt much too exposed. She had to resist the urge to cover herself up. It was silly for a lady to cover herself from her husband. Besides, the way Mic was looking at her actually made her skin tingle with a strange sensation she'd never experienced before. She wasn't sure what to make of it except that it was pleasant.

He cleared his throat and shut the door. "I'm quiet when I walk. It's a habit I picked up when I was a child. You can't track an animal if it can hear you." He turned his gaze back to her. "I know this is an odd question, but will we be," he cleared his throat, "in bed together tonight?"

"Do you want to be in bed with me?" she asked, suddenly wondering if the idea of being with her repulsed him. Perhaps if she was pretty like the women her brother had often compared her to, he wouldn't even hesitate to be with her in an intimate setting.

"Of course, I do," he said, the desire in his voice relieving her of her fears. "I'd like to make you my wife. I just want to make sure you're ready. The marriage happened so fast." His face grew bright red, and he rubbed his eyes. "If I have to keep looking at you in that chemise, I'm going to lose what little control I have and make you my wife down here."

Her eyes grew wide. Really? He wanted her—desired her—so much that he was tempted to have his way with her outside of the bedroom? And with the kerosene lamp still lit? Her heartbeat picked up in excitement. She never thought she might be so appealing to a man that he would express such a sentiment to her. She had thought her husband would be reluctant to come to her on their wedding night. More than that, she thought her husband would need complete darkness, too.

Maybe your husband will be able to overlook the fact that you're built like a boy, her brother used to taunt her. *That is, if he can get used to your face first.*

She forced aside the past. No. She wasn't going to let her brother's words ruin this night. It was just her and Mic. And she liked how he made her feel. She didn't want anything to ruin that.

In a mixture of excitement and nervousness, she went to the ladder that went to the loft. Glancing behind her, she saw that Mic was watching her with a heated gaze. Once more, her skin tingled in excitement.

Displaying far more bravado than she felt, she climbed the ladder, aware he was still watching her. She didn't know what it was about the whole thing that made her feel so powerful, but for the first time in her life, she was the one in control of a situation. She wasn't simply reacting to the events around her; she was leading them.

She reached the top of the ladder and glanced back at Mic, who hadn't budged an inch. Surprised, she asked, "Are you going to join me, or do I have to go back down there?"

At once, he darted for the ladder. She would have laughed if his urgency to be with her wasn't so thrilling. This was nice. Well, it was more than nice. It was absolutely wonderful to be desired so much that he was following her with such serious intent.

She sat on the bed right before he did. Now she couldn't help but laugh. "You sure do move fast when you decide you want something."

He wrapped his arms around her and kissed her lips, then her cheek, and then her neck. "I couldn't help it. You're just so beautiful." He lifted his head so he could look at her in the moonlight streaming in through the small window above the bed. "You're alright with me doing this, aren't you?"

She nodded. "Wasn't that obvious when I invited you up here?"

"I wanted to be sure. I've been waiting so long for this moment. I was afraid I was letting my desire get in the way of what you were really saying."

Before she had a chance to respond, he was kissing her again. They fell back onto the bed together. He settled on top of her and deepened the kiss.

This whole thing of being swept up in passion was exhilarating. She wrapped her arms around his shoulders, eager to find out where all of this was leading. She was sure it was somewhere wonderful. If simply being touched and kissed by him was heavenly, she was sure all of it was going to be thoroughly enjoyable.

His mouth left hers, and he left a trail of kisses from her neck to her breasts. Even through the fabric of her chemise, the contact sent a spark through her. He cupped her breasts in his hands, and he brought his mouth to one of her nipples. Groaning, she wrapped her legs around him. She wasn't sure where such an urge came from to do such a thing, but it seemed like an appropriate response.

He shifted so that he could slip his hands under her chemise, and, in one swift motion, he pulled the chemise over her head. After tossing it to the floor, he removed his own shirt and undershirt, and, before she had time to blink, he unbuttoned his pants and shoved them and his drawers to his knees and got back on top of her.

She thought about pointing out the fact that he still had his pants and boots on, but he started touching her breasts again. She sighed in contentment and closed her eyes, giving into the feel of his hands and mouth.

Even in his enthusiasm, he was gentle with her, and part of that was why she had no problem being with him this way. He could have taken advantage of her at any point once she was off the stagecoach, but he hadn't. He had made sure he married her, and then he made sure he had her permission before he took her to bed. That said a lot about him. It meant he was the kind of person who endeavored to do the right thing, and she liked that most about him.

When he was satisfied with exploring her breasts, he worked his way down her body until he settled between her legs. On impulse, she parted her legs further, an action which allowed him better access to anything he wanted. His mouth was gentle on her flesh. So gentle, in fact, that she was a bit ticklish as he kissed her. But then he slid a finger into her, and the ticklish sensation gave way to pleasure.

With a moan, she shifted so that he went deeper into her. She had no idea that part of her body was made to feel good. He slid another finger into her then traced her sensitive nub with his tongue. She groaned in pleasure. She could feel some pressure building up inside her, but she wasn't sure what to make of it.

She had no idea how long he spent stroking her until he got up and positioned himself between her legs so he could enter her. There was a momentary sting that broke her out of the bliss she'd been in. But that soon eased as he moved inside her.

She lifted her hips to take him deeper into her, and before long, she became aware that she enjoyed the feel of him inside her. No one had ever taken the time to explain what happened between a husband and wife in bed. Given the private nature of what she and Mic were doing, she certainly couldn't blame them. This seemed much too personal to ever share with another person.

She had no way of knowing how long he was making love to her before he grew still and moaned. She became aware of the way he throbbed inside her, and judging by the look on his face, she knew he had received pleasure from the act. Which was good because she had, too.

When he relaxed, he held her in his arms and kissed her. There was no longer the same urgency in his kissing that there had been before, but there was no doubt that he still desired her.

After some time, he slid out of her and finished taking off the rest of his things. Then he retrieved the blanket that had fallen off the bed. He settled onto his back and drew her into his arms before he placed the blanket over both of them.

She wasn't sure what to say. He probably wasn't sure what to say, either, since he remained quiet. She thought perhaps he had drifted off to sleep, but at one point, he kissed her and whispered that he was happy she was with him. Her face warmed with pleasure, and she was so excited by his proclamation that she had trouble sleeping well into the night.

Chapter Seven

Lillian woke up the next morning to the enticing aroma of food from downstairs. Still tired, she had to resist the urge to snuggle under the warm blanket and go back to sleep. In the past, she might have done that, but she no longer had a house of servants to wait on her. Now, she was married to a man who was taking care of his own piece of land, and he would probably need some help.

She sat up. Her chemise was neatly folded at the end of the bed. She was sure Mic had flung it to the floor last night. He must have retrieved it from there and placed it on the bed when he got up that morning. She wondered how it was possible she hadn't even heard him. She didn't wake up at every little sound, but she wasn't a heavy sleeper, either.

Since her trunk was still downstairs, she had no choice but to put the chemise on. Last night, it'd been dark when Mic had made love to her. She wasn't sure she wanted to go down there with so little on in the daylight. But since they were married, it was only a matter of time before he saw her not fully dressed in the daytime. She might as well get the initial time over with.

Despite her nervousness, she climbed down the ladder. Glancing over her shoulder, she saw that Mic was stirring something in the large pot on the cookstove. She couldn't tell what it was, but it smelled so good her mouth watered.

"Did you get enough rest?" Mic asked as she reached the bottom rung.

She stepped onto the floor and tried not to shy away when she noticed the way his gaze traced her body. Her skin flooded with the same warmth it had last night. He couldn't see everything through the chemise, could he? She didn't think he could, but it was hard to know for sure since he seemed as if he could.

She forced her feet forward so that she could walk over to him. "Yes, I got enough rest. What time is it?"

He gestured to the small clock on the shelf above the cookstove. "Would you believe it's almost one?"

Her jaw dropped. "In the afternoon?"

He chuckled. "Yep." He set the ladle down and wrapped his arm around her waist. Giving her a playful squeeze, he added, "You were exhausted."

"It can't be one. It has to be earlier than that."

This only made him laugh harder. "Nope. That clock is right." He drew her into his embrace. "You had a long journey. I'm sure you'll wake up earlier tomorrow." Then, he wiggled his eyebrows at her. "That is, if I let you get any sleep tonight."

Once more, there was that look in his eyes that told her he desired her. And suddenly, she didn't feel quite so shy anymore. She leaned into him and brought her lips to his. With anyone else, she didn't think she'd ever be so daring, but he had a way of making her feel comfortable enough to take risks.

In this case, the risk paid off, for he returned her kiss. His tongue brushed her lower lip, and she parted her mouth in a silent invitation for him to deepen the kiss. He let out a low moan, and she became aware of the male hardness that pressed against her abdomen. Now that she'd been in bed with him, she knew what it meant. It meant that he wanted to be with her so much that nothing else mattered.

And that was thrilling. She loved the way his hands moved over her body and the way they slid under her chemise so he could feel her bare flesh. He even pulled her more firmly up against him so that he was more intimately pressed against her. He didn't just desire her. He *needed* her.

Hoping to encourage him, she removed her chemise. When he stopped fondling her, she asked, "Did I do something wrong?" Perhaps he didn't want her to be so forward. Maybe this wasn't something women were expected to do.

When she realized that his gaze was sweeping up and down her body, it occurred to her that he'd only been taking the moment to study her in the sunlight. "Honey, you didn't do anything wrong. I was just thinking what a lucky man I am to have you here."

He swiftly unbuttoned his pants, letting her see just how much he wanted her. She supposed she should be shy and look away as he proceeded to remove the rest of his clothes, but she was fascinated to note the differences between them. He was solid strength and hard while she was all curves and soft.

He led her to the table and laid her on it before he resumed his exploration of her. Unlike last night, he took his time, as if he wished to savor every inch of her. She probably should remind him about the stew. She didn't want the food to burn, but at the moment, all she cared about was how wonderful he was making her feel. Once more, she was caught up in the bliss he'd given her last night. Right now, in this place, it was just the two of them. Nothing, and no one else, mattered.

When he entered her, she felt a pleasant sensation that started at her core and went straight to her toes. She sighed in contentment and wrapped her legs around his waist, allowing him to go deeper into her. He moaned and murmured that she felt good. He also felt good. The way he moved inside her, with slow and purposeful thrusts, brought her to an awareness of a sensitive spot deep within her. He seemed to be stroking all the right places, and as he grew more insistent in his thrusting, she felt her body growing tense, as if she was heading for something even more wonderful than what she was already experiencing.

But before she could reach her destination, he cried out and grew taut. She felt the familiar throbbing that told her he was releasing his seed into her. The action warmed her. It meant he'd received pleasure from her body, and she wanted that for him. But she wasn't sure what to make of the momentum that had been building up inside her just now. It really seemed as if it was leading to something. She just wished she knew what that something was.

When he relaxed, he leaned forward and brought her into his arms. He kissed her lips, her cheeks, and her neck in a way that told her, even if they had only met a couple of days ago, he cherished her. And that made her feel wonderful for an altogether different reason.

He gave her a lingering kiss on the lips and then smiled at her. "This is certainly a nice way to start the day."

Feeling a bit playful, she teased, "You didn't start the day this way. You were down here by the time I woke up."

He shrugged. "I might have been up since seven."

"You were up that long?"

"I'm used to getting up early, even on nights I don't get much sleep. Plus, I was excited about being married to you. It's nice to have someone to share this place with me, and it's even better that you happen to be a beautiful woman."

"You really think I'm beautiful?"

"Of course, I do. I wouldn't have been so consumed with desire last night and just now if you weren't. The male part of me doesn't lie. If it likes the way a woman looks, it makes no secret about it." He gave her a wicked smile. "You did happen to notice it, didn't you?"

"It's hard not to notice something that goes inside me."

"Well, when I'm erect, it means I like what I see."

He kissed her again, this time making it short and playful, but it thrilled her all the same. He really did think she was beautiful. He hadn't just been saying it. Not that he struck her as the kind of person who would say something he didn't mean, but it was nice to have his opinion of her validated.

He eased off of her and helped her to her feet. Then he took her chemise. "Do you wear this during the day under your clothes?"

Since she nodded, he helped her into it. Then he quickly put on his clothes, and as he did so, she took a moment to study him. She rather liked knowing that he grew erect because he was attracted to her. Maybe it was silly, but she decided the penis was her favorite part of his body, though she'd never come out and actually tell him that.

He went back over to the cookstove, picked up the ladle, and stirred the contents in the pot. "I'm making stew. I'm using vegetables from the garden and deer meat that I kept preserved in the cellar." He set the ladle down and returned to her. "I'll serve it when you're done getting dressed." He gestured to the trunk. "Do you have anything in there that's suitable for life out here?"

"Well, I'm not even sure what life out here is all about."

"You mind if I look in there? I can tell you if you have anything that's good to wear or not."

She shook her head, so he went to the trunk and lifted the lid. She shifted from one foot to the other. Was now a good time to mention the money she'd hidden? Or should she wait until the timing was better? She'd have to explain why the money was there, and doing that would require her to go into how things were with her brother and Robert. It wasn't exactly a conversation someone could have with someone in five minutes. Not unless she said that she could answer his questions later. Surely, he was bound to have questions. If she found out he had money hidden in his trunk, she'd want to know why, and that would lead to lots of questions. Questions that would take at least a good hour to answer.

He sorted through her clothes. "Some of these will be alright out here. Your fancier clothes will be better suited for winter when it's cold. The trees protect us from the wind, but we'll get more snow than they will in town."

Curious since she didn't think she had packed anything fancy, she went over to him. "Which clothes do you think are fancy?"

He pulled out a shirtwaist and gestured to the green heavy dress she'd packed for cooler weather. She didn't see what was so fancy about it. Back in Virginia, it was so plain that she'd only worn it around the house. She wouldn't have dared to be seen in public in something so simple.

"I heard women dress a lot better back East than they do out here," he said. "So I'm not surprised. Around here, an outfit like that would cost at least a month's wages. I bet it's cheaper back there since you have all the materials right where you are to make dresses. You don't have to order them in a catalogue."

"Oh, well, I didn't make these," she slowly replied. "I don't know how to sew anything. I do some embroidery, but that's only for decorations. But I'm willing to learn."

"I can make belts and boots, but Abby's the one who makes clothes. Usually, we order the material in a catalogue at the mercantile. Most of the time, we keep patching up old clothes. I can do some mending. Your clothes are excellent quality. You won't need to do any mending for a long time. It's a good thing Abby didn't see these. She would have gotten jealous to see such fine things."

He set the clothes back in the trunk and shut the lid.

"Let's get this trunk upstairs," he said. "Then you can put the clothes wherever you want them in the dresser." He lifted it then paused. "I hate to ask for help, but it's heavier than I thought it'd be. Would you mind holding onto the handle over here?" He nodded to the side of the trunk. "You can climb the ladder first so that the bulk of the weight will be on my end."

Since he looked expectantly at her, she took the handle from the side of the trunk and led him to the ladder. The trunk was harder to get up to the loft than she'd expected, but once it was there, she actually felt safer. The money would be harder to find…should someone snoop through the cabin.

"I brought up a pitcher of fresh water this morning," Mic told her, directing her attention to the item on the dresser, which was next to an empty bowl and clean cloth. "When you're done washing up and getting dressed, the stew will be ready to eat. Then I can show you around outside."

"Thanks, Mic," she whispered, touched by his thoughtfulness. He was so unlike anyone she'd ever met.

With a smile, he kissed her. "I'll miss you."

Finding it amusing that he should say such a thing, she laughed. "I'm going to be right here."

"I know, but it's more fun having you right next to me." He kissed her again then headed down the ladder.

She had to bend down, but she could see him go to the cookstove. Still amused, she straightened back up and got ready for the day.

Chapter Eight

Mic was whistling as he set the bowls of stew on the table. He knew having a wife would be a good thing, but he had no idea just how wonderful it'd be. Now the aching loneliness that had been a part of his life ever since he'd had to make a home on this property was gone. Better yet, his wife happened to have a sweet disposition. Even better was the fact that she was beautiful.

He heard Lillian descend the ladder and glanced up in time to see her dressed in a skirt that was a deep shade of brown and a cream-colored shirtwaist. Her boots had sharp heels in them, and he suddenly wondered if they would make it difficult for her to walk outside. In the cabin, she'd be fine, but on the uneven ground with tree roots jutting out here and there, she might end up tripping all the time.

"Do you have any boots that have less of a heel in them?" he asked her.

She paused halfway down the ladder. "These are the boots that have the smallest heel on them."

That's what he was afraid of. "My mother had a pair of moccasins. They're in the loft. Those boots will be fine in the cabin, but they're going to give you some problems outside."

"What are moccasins?"

"Flat shoes made of leather. They're a lot more comfortable than the boots you're wearing." He stepped over to her so she could see the ones he was wearing. "They look like this."

She lowered her gaze. "Oh. I think I saw some of those in a store window in one of the small towns I stopped in while I was traveling up here. I thought they were for wearing in the house."

"You can wear them inside, but they're good for outside, too. I wore a pair of boots when I went to get you from the stagecoach, and I wear those if I have to go to town. But when I'm here, I like to be comfortable."

"Alright. I'll wear the ones your mother owned. Where are they?"

"I'll show you where they are."

With a nod, she headed back up the ladder. He headed on up after her, and as he did, he realized he got a glimpse up her skirt. A smile crossed his face. He might have to insist she always climb the ladder before he did. It was certainly nice to be at this vantage point.

He shook his head. He had no idea his mind would stray so much to matters of an intimate nature when he brought her to his cabin. It was definitely good he'd talked Jeremiah into coming along so he could marry them.

Once he was in the loft with her, he went to the small trunk in the corner. He had tucked it away with other items that belonged to Wade and Abby. These were all things that belonged to the past. It was a reminder of how things had been before Charles ruined Wade's life and made outlaws of them. And these were things he'd rather not dwell on, so he moved them aside to get to his mother's trunk. He opened it and sorted through her old clothes until he found the moccasins.

After he put them on the floor, he picked up one of the deerskin dresses. It was faded with time, but it might fit Lillian. He lifted the dress out of the trunk and showed it to her.

"What do you think of this?" he asked. "It might be more comfortable when the days get hot next month."

She took it from him and brought the top of the dress to her neck. The bottom of the dress ended at her knees. "Where's the rest of the outfit?"

He caught himself chuckling. "That is the outfit."

"But it doesn't reach my ankles. I'll end up showing my legs."

"What's wrong with that?"

"Well…" She stared at him for a moment as if she couldn't believe he even had to ask the question. Then she blurted out, "What if someone stops by and sees me? If I'm wearing this, I'll be practically naked."

"First of all, no one else lives around here for miles. And second, showing off those nice, long legs of yours is exactly why I think you should wear it." He wiggled his eyebrows at her. "You don't have to wear anything under the dress, either."

She gasped. "I could never do such a thing. Not in the day."

"You did it just now in the chemise when I was cooking the stew."

"I went down there to get clothes. I didn't have anything up here."

"Hmm… So you're telling me I should have kept your trunk down there."

She gasped again but laughed and nudged him in the shoulder. "You can't be serious. One of these days, Abby, Wade, or Jeremiah is likely to come by. I can't risk going down there in nothing but a chemise."

"Which is why you should wear that dress." He gestured to the deerskin dress she was still holding. "They won't think anything of it. Around here, the Indian women wear those all the time. Some are in their tribe and some in town. It's not like what you're used to."

She bit her lower lip and studied the dress. "I don't know. There's nothing to this thing. It even has short sleeves. My arms would also be exposed."

"Again, I can't think of one single reason for you not to wear it." He closed the trunk then picked up the moccasins and showed them to her. "It looks like these things will fit you. Why don't you try them on and see if they do? If it turns out they don't, then we know you're not meant to wear them."

"I suppose that will work."

"If the dress doesn't fit, we'll just hem up your skirt so you're more comfortable."

She shook her head at him. "I think all you want is to put me in something where I have to show a lot of my body off."

"I do. I won't deny it." He pulled her into his arms and kissed her. "The less clothes you wear, the easier it'll be for me to pull up your skirt or dress and have my way with you."

Though she groaned, he noted her amusement. "You're horrible, Mic. I had no idea that coming out here meant that I would be asked to be naked all the time. But," she added before he could say anything, "I'll try your mother's dress on tomorrow. It takes a lot of time for me to get dressed in my clothes." She gestured to what she was wearing. "And before you say it, I'm well aware that I'm giving you yet another reason to want me in your mother's dress."

He laughed. She was quick on her feet with comebacks. He liked that. It was nice to have someone who could match him in wit.

She removed her boots and then slipped the moccasins on. "They feel nice."

"I thought you might like them."

"I do. And they fit."

"If you like those, just wait until you feel how comfortable it is in the deerskin dress."

"How can you know it's comfortable? Did you wear it?"

Noting the teasing tone in her voice, he said, "My mother and Abby both swear that kind of dress is much better than what you have on. Come on. I want you to eat your stew before it gets cold. Then I want to show you around the property."

She set the deerskin dress on one of the hooks and then followed him down to the ladder.

***

After a late lunch, Lillian joined Mic and went to the barn. He showed her the milking cow that was in the stall. Then he showed her the henhouse and lifted the small door in the back so she could see the eggs the hens had just laid.

"I'll get those eggs later," he said as he secured the door. "You have to be careful because a coyote or fox might come around and get into the henhouse. That's why I have some traps set out around here." He motioned to them. "Be careful when you step through here, alright?"

She nodded. He didn't have to tell her twice! The last thing she needed was to get her foot stuck in a metal trap. The thing had jagged edges that looked painful.

"I'll take you to the garden," he said as he took her hand and led her around the henhouse.

They passed the barn, and she saw the horse eating some hay in the fenced area in the back.

"There are so many trees around here that I had to put the garden all the way out there so the sun could get to it," he added.

He pointed to a fenced-in area about half a mile from them. Not only was the sunlight able to hit the entire area, but the ground was flat, too. She glanced over her shoulder. She hadn't realized the cabin and barn were surrounded by so many trees. Well, she'd been tired by the time she came here last night. She supposed it was to be expected that she hadn't noticed quite a few things.

"The good news is that the river isn't too far from it," he continued. "It makes it easy to water the food I'm growing. We had some of the vegetables in the stew. I collected those this morning. I preserve whatever I don't eat and put it in the cellar. I'll show you the cellar later." He squeezed her hand. "Don't worry, I'll stay next to you the whole time. It's not exactly the kind of place for a lady."

"Why not? Is there something terrible in it?"

"It's a hole in the ground, and it has a lot of creeping bugs in there."

She shivered. "I'm glad you warned me."

He chuckled and squeezed her hand again. "I won't let anything crawl on you."

"Good because I don't want a bug anywhere near me."

Though, she didn't know how that could be avoided all the way out here. She'd stand a better chance of avoiding bugs if she was in town. Already, she'd noted flies in the barn and around the horse. But, with a glance at Mic, she supposed some bugs were a small price to pay if she could be with someone as sweet and charming as him. Their marriage was so hasty, she wondered if she was supposed to regret it. She didn't. Not by a long shot. But maybe others might criticize her for giving her body…and her heart…to him as fast as she had.

They reached the rectangular fenced-in area which had a surprising abundance of fruits and vegetables. He had muskmelons, strawberries, cherry tomatoes, blueberries, carrots, celery, radishes, cucumbers, peppers, broccoli, and… Her eyes stopped and went back to the broccoli. There hadn't been any of that in the stew. She glanced at Mic as he opened the latch on the fence.

"I have something to tell you, and I'm not sure you'll like it," she warned him.

He stepped into the garden and picked up two watering cans. "What is it? Did an animal get one of the fruits or vegetables? I thought I secured the area."

"No, it's not that." She turned to face him as he went over to her. "It's the broccoli. No matter how many different ways I've had that prepared for me, I don't like it." She winced. "Do you mind if I don't eat that?" Hoping she didn't upset him, she hurried to add, "I can eat everything else."

He chuckled. "I don't care if you eat broccoli or not. Wade hates that stuff. He always said I'm strange because I like it."

She relaxed. "You don't mind?"

"Of course not." He set his hand on the small of her back and kissed her. "I have plenty of things to choose from. As long as you don't go hungry, that's all that matters."

What a relief. Her parents had made her sit at the table until she ate it, and her brother would make fun of her for being picky about something as simple as what was on her plate. She didn't want to eat another piece of broccoli for as long as she lived.

"I'll get some water at the river and be right back," Mic said then headed for it.

Now she was happier than ever that she'd married Mic. She didn't know if Charles would have insisted she eat broccoli. From the way Mic made Charles sound, he probably would have. But Mic wasn't like that. He wasn't like her brother or Robert, either. He was letting her make choices. Yes, he'd taken her from the stagecoach, but he hadn't forced her to marry him. He'd asked her. Then he asked her if he could be with her in bed last night. And now he was letting her decide what she wanted to eat or not eat. She'd never been given choices before. It was nice. For the first time in her life, she had a say in what she did.

When he returned, she followed him into the garden. He set the watering cans down. "I usually go through here and pull out weeds before I water the fruits and vegetables. I'll show you the difference between a weed and the food that hasn't matured yet. When I was a boy, I made the mistake of pulling out newly growing plants. Needless to say, my poor ma had to go into her garden and plant everything all over again."

"Was she angry?"

"She was, but she was angry with herself for asking me to weed the garden without showing me what the weeds were first. She was so busy with Abby that she didn't even think about it. She had assumed Wade would teach me the difference because we went out together." He shrugged. "I don't think it occurred to her that two boys who are in a hurry to get back to playing are rushing through a chore so fast that the older one doesn't think to show the younger one what to do."

Noting the chuckle in his voice, she said, "You seem to have a good sense of humor about it."

"Well, I learned long ago that I can either find the humor in things or not. Wade tends to take things too seriously. Jeremiah does, too. Watching them all of my life made me decide to only dwell on the big things. There's enough sorrow and hardships in this world. There's no sense in letting something as small as weeds bring me down. Come. I'll show you how to tell a weed from a plant."

They spent the next fifteen minutes going through the garden. There were some spots where the stems were too small, so he said they would wait for those to grow out some more. Afterwards, she helped him water the garden.

"Are you bored yet?" he asked when they returned the empty watering cans to their usual spot.

At first, she thought he was serious, but then she caught the mischievous glint in his eyes and chuckled. "If I were bored, what would you do about it?" she replied, deciding to challenge him.

His eyebrows rose in interest. "Do you really want to know?"

She nodded, wondering what he'd come up with.

His lips curled up into a wicked grin, and before she knew it, he had swooped her up into his arms.

"Where are you taking me?" she asked.

"You'll see."

"You're not going to tell me?"

"If I did that, it wouldn't be a surprise," he began, "and if it's not a surprise, you might get bored."

He started to head back in the direction of the cabin, but then, probably because he was hoping to surprise her, he turned around and started walking to the river.

She gasped. "You can't be serious!" Surely, he wasn't going to do what she suspected he was going to do.

"I can't be serious about what?" he asked as a chuckle rose up in his throat.

"You're not going to throw me in there, are you?"

"Do you know how to swim?"

"Well, yes, but I don't want to."

"Isn't swimming fun?"

"It is if I'm in the mood for it, but I'm not in the mood for it." She tried to scramble out of his arms, but his hold on her was too secure. "I'm not bored, Mic. There's no need to throw me into the river."

She thought this might do the trick. She was wrong. He proceeded to the edge of the river and stepped into it.

"You're not really going to do this," she insisted. "I'll get all wet."

"If you get wet, that means you'll need to take your clothes off." He wiggled his eyebrows. "That would make things interesting, wouldn't it?"

"But," she protested as he stepped further into the river, "these clothes will need to dry. Won't that take a long time?"

"It's a nice day. The clothes won't take long to dry. An hour. Two at the most."

He was really going to do this. He was going to put her into the water, and there was nothing she could say or do to stop him. He waded into the water until it was halfway up to his waist and then released her. Having anticipated this, she held onto him.

He looked down at her in surprise. "So, that's how you're going to play. Alright."

He secured her in his embrace then dove into the water, taking her with him. He swam forward and then brought her back up to the surface of the water with him.

She wiped the water from her eyes and laughed. "I'll never tell you I'm bored. I promise!"

He kissed her. "I'm going to make every day fun so you don't regret marrying me."

"I have a feeling I'll never regret that." He was allowing her freedoms to do things she'd never done before. That alone was worth being here with him. The fact that he was funny and sweet just made her more grateful to be with him.

He gave her another kiss, this one much more wonderful than the previous one.

When the kiss ended, she laughed. "I can't believe we're doing this."

"Why not? It's a hot day, and the current is gentle. There's no danger of us floating away from home."

She looked in the direction of the cabin. From this vantage point, she could barely make it out. The trees obscured most of it. She could, however, make out the barn, the henhouse, and, of course the garden.

He squeezed her. "Want to take a swim?"

"I can't swim in these clothes. I'd need a bathing suit."

"Who says you need anything on? We can take our clothes off and swim."

"Mic, you're impossible. There's no way we can do that."

"There's no one but us around here. It's not like we're going to swim a long distance. It'll just be a little bit that way." He nodded in one direction. "Then a little bit over there." He nodded in the opposite direction. "It'll be fun. I have an idea. I'll run back to the cabin and grab a bar of soap and a couple of towels. I bet you could use a bath after all the traveling you've done."

She would like a bath. Back in Virginia, she'd taken one almost every day. And he was right. She hadn't taken one since she'd paid for one at the hotel in a South Dakota town. "Alright," she agreed.

"Great." He kissed her again and then led her to the shoreline. "While you get undressed, I'll gather the bathing supplies. I'll be back in a few minutes."

By the way he hurried to the cabin, she had a nagging suspicion he planned to do more than bathe and swim with her. With a chuckle, she proceeded to remove her wet clothes.

Chapter Nine

A few days later, Mic took Lillian through the wooded area. He had meant to set the traps sooner, but he'd gotten distracted by helping her do the laundry, show her how to make a couple of meals, and take care of the animals. He wasn't quite sure what her background was like, but he'd deducted that it was much different from this life. He didn't want her to regret coming out here with him. His mother had grown up in this wilderness. She was used to the demands it put on a person. Lillian, however, had lived a gentle life back East. So it was important he take the time to teach her what she needed to know. And now that she had the basics down, he could go on to other things.

When they came near one of his favorite trapping spots, he stopped and whispered, "A lot of animals come through here. You can see their tracks." He pointed to the footprints from a variety of critters. "These are good areas to put a trap."

She nodded then asked, "Why are you whispering?"

He paused for a moment. "I'm so used to being quiet through here that it seemed appropriate to whisper," he replied in a louder voice. "My parents taught me to be as quiet as a ghost through these parts. You never know when a food source is up ahead. It can mean the difference between life and death if you make a noise that startles an animal."

"I had wondered why you were so quiet when you walked. I never hear you coming."

"Have I scared you?"

"Sometimes."

He offered her a comforting smile. "I'm sorry. It wasn't my intention to scare you."

"I know. That's why I never got upset."

"I should teach you how to walk like a ghost. Then you can scare me."

She laughed and kissed him. It was nice whenever she kissed him. She'd been shy about initiating any kind of romantic sentiment at first, but she was slowly warming up to it. And he certainly wasn't going to do anything to dissuade her.

"Let me set the first trap, and then I'll show you how to walk so quietly that no one can hear you." He set down the traps then cleared the leaves from the area he liked to set his foot trap. "I like to use different traps. Some are designed to catch small animals and others are for larger ones. I even have some holes dug out further that way." He gestured to the north. "A year ago, I learned that having different traps bettered my chances of survival. As you noticed, I have a lot of meat. If I had to rely on the garden, I wouldn't last long out here."

"It's not like you have any place to purchase food around here."

"No, I don't. It's far removed from anything and anyone."

Which was exactly what he'd needed after he'd unsuccessfully tried to help Wade fend off Charles that night when Charles took over Wade's ranch. It'd only been him and Wade against Charles and nine men. The numbers had been too stacked against them. Looking back, he should have known staying in the house wasn't going to do any good. They hadn't even been able to save Wade's family. Once Charles had forced them off, Charles had branded the two as outlaws.

Even now, they weren't prepared to go up against Charles and his men, but they needed to get Wade's son out of there. It was bad enough Wade's wife was no longer alive. They couldn't risk harm coming to the boy, too. But they needed a plan. A good one. Which was why he had to wait for Abby and Wade to come tell him when the time was right.

Turning his attention back to the foot trap, he removed the pair of gloves he had in his back pocket. "I should teach you how to set this in case you ever need to do it."

As he suspected, Lillian looked apprehensive. "You think I'll need to do this in the future?"

He shrugged. "I don't know if you will or not. I fully plan on doing it, but if something were to happen to me and you needed to hunt for food, knowing what to do will come in handy."

She seemed as if she was searching for a suitable argument, but he knew there wasn't one. They were the only two people out here. It was up to them to survive. Sure, she could take a horse, but she didn't know her way to town. He'd purposely chosen a location that was hard to track. He'd left hints on how to get to this place, but unless someone knew exactly what those were, they wouldn't find it.

But what if something happened and she had to go to town? What if she needed to find her way back? He hadn't realized that taking a wife could possibly put her in a sensitive situation. He'd let his loneliness override any of the arguments Jeremiah and Wade had given him when he told them he intended to marry Charles' mail-order bride. Now, he wondered if he'd unwittingly put her in harm's way. Yes, he was safe from Charles and the men out here. No one would find them. But what if something happened to him when he helped Wade get his son back?

"Lillian, come here." He patted the spot next to him.

She knelt beside him.

"Before I show you how to set the trap, I should explain something. It's important that no one find us, at least not until my name is cleared. Since Charles and his men chased Wade and me out of town, he had us branded as outlaws. He's friends with the marshal, and the marshal is the mayor's brother. Neither one of them are respectable men. Anyway, the bounty on our heads is enough that some are searching for me and Wade."

"Do you need money so you're not outlaws anymore?"

"No. The bounty is what a man will get if he catches us alive or dead. Wade's by himself, and I'm here. We thought it safer to separate out in the side of this mountain. Until we can set things right, we'll continue to be outlaws, but we have to be careful about it and we have to be patient."

"What Charles did was terrible. It's even more terrible that men who are supposed to uphold the law have joined him."

"There are always going to be bad people who'll do whatever they want, and the law often doesn't hold them accountable." He kissed her. "It's necessary to take precautions." He looked up at the trees. "Lillian, I marked the trees from town to my cabin. Then, for good measure, I marked all of the nearby trees. If something happens to me when Wade and I go for his son, it's important that you're able to find your way home. I cut each tree. The cabin is that way." He pointed to the southwest. Then he pointed to the tree nearest them. "Do you see the cut halfway up that trunk?" He motioned to the cut he'd made. "The left side is lower than the right. That means the cabin is to the southwest of here. On our way here, the cabin was northeast of where we left the shack that day we got married. I started marking the trees. The right side is higher than the left. That means you go up the path. If you can stay with the trees that are marked, you'll be able to find your way to the cabin. I should take you back to the shack and lead you to the cabin so you know what to look for. There are other markers along the way."

"You think something is going to happen to you?"

"I can't tell what the future will bring. I'm not planning for anything bad to happen, but I never dreamt Charles would steal

Wade's ranch, kill Wade's wife, and steal Wade's son." Noting the worry in her eyes, he squeezed her shoulders. "I intend to enjoy every moment we have together, but I need to make sure you'll be alright."

Not wishing to worry her further, he showed her how to set the trap. He would let her set the next one. It was one thing to see the process being done. It was another to do it. When she set the trap, she would remember it better. She'd also be more comfortable doing it in the future.

Once he finished, he put the leaves around the trap to hide it from the animals. "You want the trap exposed, but you don't want the animal to see it," he explained.

He straightened up then pulled off his gloves and shoved them back into his pocket. He picked up the rest of the traps and took her hand.

"If you're going to walk without being heard, you need to be purposeful," he said. "After you do this for as long as I have, it'll come naturally, but for now, go slow and watch where you're going. You don't want to step on any twigs. You can step on leaves, but try not to step on the dry ones. Dry leaves will make a crinkling sound if you do, and that could give you away. Fortunately, most of the leaves are soft."

He let go of her hand and took a few steps ahead of her to demonstrate the best way she should walk. He stopped and turned to face her. After he gestured for her to try it, she took a tentative step forward then paused. She glanced around as if she expected something to jump out at her.

"Keep on going," he encouraged, hiding his amusement in case she lost her nerve and didn't want to keep practicing.

She took a few more steps, and on one, a twig snapped, echoing through the air. She jerked back as if it'd been a gunshot.

He offered her a comforting smile. "Everything sounds louder than it should when we're quiet. If you stay still and listen, you'll be surprised by how much you hear."

She nodded. Then, she studied the ground in front of her before closing the distance between them. She stepped over two dry leaves, but considering how quiet she'd been otherwise, he thought she did a wonderful job.

He put his free arm around her shoulders and kissed her. "You did great. We'll keep on practicing. Before you know it, you'll be walking through here without making a single sound."

"I don't know if I'll ever get as good as you, but I'll do my best."

"I bet you can do it. You just need to believe in yourself." He took her hand, and they continued to practice walking in silence.

***

Lillian knew it was silly, but her heart wouldn't stop hammering in her chest as she picked up the cooking gloves from the table. This was her second attempt at cooking something on her own. The other day, she'd made soup, which was a relatively easy meal. Today, she was baking coyote meat. Since Mic had caught and skinned the animal, she felt it was only fair she try her hand at cooking it. She wanted to do her part in helping him around the place.

In the month since she'd come here, she was already forgetting her old life. Today, she was even wearing the deerskin dress. It a little loose on her, but it suited her just fine, and as Mic had promised, she was cooler in it. She didn't wear it when they went out to set traps because she didn't want to get her legs or arms dirty, but it was perfect for household work.

She checked the clock on the wall above the cook stove. Mic had told her it would be ready in another minute. She tapped her foot on the floor as she waited for the hand on the clock to hit the next minute. She really hoped this turned out right. It smelled good through the cabin. That meant there was a good chance she'd done this right. Mic had told her as long as there wasn't smoke coming out from the oven, she was alright. She checked the oven door. There didn't seem to be any smoke coming from it.

She glanced up at the clock again. Good! It was time.

She slipped on the gloves. They were Mic's so they were big, but she was careful to keep them on as she opened the oven door. She backed away for a moment, just in case a large billow of smoke came out at her. But, thankfully, it didn't.

She stepped closer and saw the gravy she'd help Mic make bubbling on top of the meat that was in the pan. Everything looked like it should.

Encouraged, she got a firm hold on the pan and pulled it out of the oven. She set the pan on top of the cook stove and shut the oven door. She inspected the meat again, this time taking a moment to inhale the aroma. Her mouth watered in anticipation. She hoped this tasted as good as it smelled.

She took off the gloves and set them on the table. Then she finished making the salad. Cutting up vegetables from the garden was easy. That didn't require any instructions beyond, "Here's the knife."

Anyone watching her would probably think she was silly to be so excited about cooking, but it was the first time she'd ever done anything on her own, besides escape Virginia on a train and arrange for the stagecoach ride out to the Wyoming wilderness. All of her life, servants had done stuff for her. She hadn't had a reason to do anything herself.

Now, however, she did. In fact, there were a lot of things she could do herself. Except for cooking, Mic had been with her for all the chores that needed to be done around the place.

Eventually, she would do more things on her own, but she was glad he was taking the time to show her what to do.

The more she got to know him, the happier she was she'd married him. Thank goodness she hadn't ended up with Charles. Charles was just like Robert. She shivered.

That was all in the past. Out here, it was just her and Mic, and she liked that just fine.

The door opened, and Mic came into the cabin with a pail of fresh milk. "It smells good in here."

She finished cutting her carrot and then put it in with the salad. "I think the meat actually turned out well." She gestured to the pan. "What do you think?"

He set the pail on the table and looked in the pan. "Can I have a knife and fork?"

With a nod, she retrieved the items he requested and gave them to him.

He cut into the meat and inspected it. "I like meat that's brown all the way through. I ate meat that wasn't cooked all the way once and got sick. Ever since, I make sure there's no pink. Well, a little pink is alright, but I don't dare do more than that."

"I don't want to get sick, either. Did I cook it long enough?"

"Yep." He indicated for her to look at the middle of the roast, and sure enough, it was brown all the way through. "It's perfect."

"Really? You're not just saying that because you know it's what I want to hear, are you?"

He chuckled and set the knife and fork aside. "I wouldn't take a chance and lie about something that might make me sick. You did good."

She clapped her hands. "I had no idea cooking could be easy."

"Well, I wouldn't say all of it is easy. There are some things that require a lot of steps to make. I happen to avoid those meals, so you have nothing to worry about."

She supposed since he'd been a single man living here by himself and had so much to do that he would pick easy meals to cook. That was just as well. It meant he would be happy with the meals she made, and that's what mattered.

"This evening, I'm going to pack some things so we can make that trip to town. We won't actually go into town. I'll take you far enough so you can see the trail that leads to the trees. From there, the paths separate out like they did after we took you from the stagecoach. You should know how to get from town to this cabin."

"Do you really think I'll need to know that?" He'd mentioned it before, but that was a couple weeks ago. She thought he had changed his mind about it.

"I don't know if you'll need to know how to get back here or not, but it's better to be safe than sorry."

She knew he was right, but she'd rather not think about it. She'd rather assume nothing bad was ever going to happen to either one of them.

He cupped her face in his hands. "I have every intention of growing old with you."

"I know," she whispered.

He smiled at her. "It's nice to know you'd miss me if I wasn't around."

"Of course, I'd miss you. I like being with you."

"I like being with you, too." He lowered his head and kissed her. "You're a part of me now. I'll do everything I can to make sure no one ever separates us."

"You'd better," she joked, feeling better.

He chuckled and kissed her again. "I don't take any chances unless I think I can make it out alive." He brushed her cheeks with the pads of his thumbs. "You really are a beautiful woman."

Heart warm, she returned his smile.

He let go of her face and patted the small of her back. "I'll set the table while you finish the salad, alright?"

She nodded and turned back to cutting the rest of the vegetables.

Chapter Ten

"That's Laramie," Mic told Lillian as he took in the bustling town north of them.

They sat on his horse, and he had his arm wrapped around her waist. On impulse, he kissed her neck.

She giggled. "I don't think you're all that interested in the town."

"I'm not," he admitted. "I'm more interested in you. I see no reason to hide it."

"I'm glad you don't. I like knowing you enjoy being with me."

"Being with you is the best thing that's ever happened to me. I was lonely before you came into my life. I just didn't realize how lonely I was until I met you."

"I've never been happier than the moment you came into my life. Though," she hurried to amend, "I was scared at first. I wasn't sure what you, Abby, Jeremiah, and Wade planned to do with me."

"I figured you were scared. I was hoping that if Abby was there, you'd feel better. Plus, Abby wouldn't have wanted to miss the action. She's not the type who likes to stay at home."

"Considering what she told me, I figured as much. I imagine that she spends her days out hunting for wild game and wrestling rattlesnakes."

Lillian's assessment of his sister made him laugh. "She's not happy being a teacher. She took the job because it means she didn't have to get married."

"She doesn't want to marry?"

"She doesn't want to marry any of the men in town. Most of them gamble or drink too often, and she's not interested in marrying someone in the army. Being a teacher, she's forbidden to get married, so it keeps all of the bachelors away."

"Certainly, she'll want to get married at some point."

He shrugged. "I don't know if she'll want to get married or not. She loves the freedom of doing whatever she wants. Granted, she doesn't let the school board know what she does in her free time. She's discreet. They would never approve of her acting so much like a man, but Wade and I feel much better knowing she can take care of herself. Life out here can be rough, especially on a single woman."

"How is it rough out here? From what I've seen, it's not that bad. Sure, cooking and washing take up a lot of time, but I wouldn't call it rough."

"That's not the kind of rough I mean. As I said, a lot of those men in town gamble and drink. That leads to a lot of gunfights. Women and children don't go out past dark. Yes, the army's nearby, but they're too busy dealing with the Indians to care about what's happening in town."

"Where I come from, it was rough, too."

Surprised since she hadn't said much about where she came from, he gave her waist an encouraging squeeze. "How was it rough there?"

"Well, I grew up in a much more affluent area than this. I'm sure you could tell that by my clothes."

"Yes, I could." Also, he'd had to teach her how to cook and clean. Obviously, she'd had servants.

She cleared her throat. "Anyway, the men in Virginia also gambled and drank. They just did it in elite clubs where only the best of the best were allowed to be members. They didn't always gamble for money. Sometimes they wagered businesses and people they had control over."

Surprised, he asked, "People they had control over?"

"Sisters, daughters…sometimes even wives. The only thing was that no one ever spoke publicly about it. On the surface, everything was respectable, but we all knew it was going on. We just didn't say anything as long as the men were discreet."

"Were you one of the people who were wagered?"

She swallowed the lump in her throat and nodded. "I try not to think about it."

He was about to tell her not to think about it because it obviously caused her pain, but he wanted to know what had happened. He brushed some of her hair back and set his head on her shoulder. Then he wrapped his other arm around her. "Would you tell me? Just this once. I won't ask about it ever again."

"As I said, many men gambled. My brother was one of them. He lost all of his money to Robert. It turned out Robert cheated, but the men who witnessed the game refused to admit it. Robert had too much influence." She shrugged. "Since my brother didn't have the money to pay him, he offered me and my dowry. Robert only accepted it because my dowry was a lot and because it would give him a connection to the Van Horn estate. My real name is Prudence Van Horn. Are you familiar with the name Van Horn?"

"No. I don't think anyone out here is familiar with that name."

"For some reason I thought everyone knew that name. It was why I hid under the alias Lillian Christian. I also did it so Robert wouldn't track me down. I was afraid if anyone out here realized I was Prudence Van Horn, they would use me for their gain."

"You think they would have taken you back to Robert?"

"Either that or take the money I brought with me."

"You brought money with you?"

"I took my dowry and ran off with it the day before I was supposed to marry Robert. I hid it throughout my trunk in secret compartments. When you and the others stopped the stagecoach, I thought you were coming for the money or to sell me to Robert. I didn't realize you were trying to stop me from marrying Charles until you said so."

"We only came to stop you from marrying Charles because we knew what he'd do to you. He would've been cruel, and we didn't want an innocent woman to suffer just because she stumbled into something she didn't know about. We had no idea you were Prudence Van Horn or that you had money in your trunk."

"I'm glad you four came when you did. It sounds as if Charles and Robert are alike. They both think they own other people and can get whatever they want. I wouldn't have wanted to end up with someone like that."

He squeezed her waist. "Then it's a good thing we came along when we did."

"Mic, I like the name Lillian. It's my middle one, and I always preferred it to Prudence. Would you keep calling me Lillian?"

"Sure." He kissed her neck. "To me, you'll always be Lillian. That's the person I fell in love with."

"You love me?"

He chuckled. "Can't you tell?"

"Well, it's different when I hear you say it."

"In that case, I love you."

"I love you, too."

Warmth spread across his body at hearing the words, and he understood why she wanted to hear them. It was one thing to hug and kiss someone, but knowing you were loved by them was even more pleasant.

"I'll keep your secret safe," he promised. "No one has to know."

"Thank you."

"I'm just glad you're here with me. I don't want to live without you."

His gaze went to the town, and he saw where Wade's ranch was on the outskirts of it. Charles was there for the time being. That couldn't be helped. But one day, he, Abby, and Jeremiah would help Wade get it back. First, they needed to get Wade's son to safety. After that, they could make plans to take the ranch back.

God willing, they would all live through it because he meant what he had told Lillian: he didn't want to live without her. He didn't care what her past was. The money and family name meant nothing to him. All that mattered was who she was and that she was his wife.

He kissed her again. "Now that you know where the town is, I'll show you how to get back to the cabin." He turned the horse around and went down the trail that would take them to the trees in the side of the mountain.

***

That night, Mic and Lillian camped a couple miles past the cabin where they had gotten married. She was snuggled up to Mic in the bedroll they were sharing. Though the day had been a long one, she couldn't sleep.

After she'd told Mic the truth about her past, she thought things might change between them. She'd grown up with all the material things a person could ever want, and he went without many of the comforts life had to offer. She thought he might not understand why she took her money and ran away from Robert.

But he had understood, and that was a relief. Now there were no secrets between them. And he loved her anyway.

Her mind unwittingly went to Millie. Millie's life had been more like Mic's. She'd had to sew her own clothes and make things like butter. There had even been a time in Millie's life when grasshoppers had eaten her family's crops, and as a result, they'd lost their home. They'd had to live in a makeshift tent until they could get back on their feet.

How could Lillian compare her situation to that? In the end, she decided not to tell Millie anything about her life for fear that Millie would criticize her for leaving her lavish lifestyle behind. After all, Lillian had never been through anything as harsh as what Millie had gone through.

She glanced at the stars. She hoped Millie was happy at her new teaching position in Medicine Bow.

"It's hard to sleep when you're used to a bed, isn't it?" Mic asked.

She lifted her head. "I thought you were asleep."

"I think I dozed off for a while, but I heard you sighing and woke up." He brushed her cheek with his thumb. "Are you sad about something?"

"Not sad exactly." She paused as she tried to think of the right words to express how she was feeling. "It's just that what I went through in Virginia is nothing like what other people go through. I mean, Wade lost his family and his ranch. I came here with a young woman who'd had nights where she didn't know if she was going to have anything to eat or a house to sleep in." She shrugged and broke eye contact with him. "It just doesn't seem like being told you're going to marry someone who only wants your money is all that bad when you put things in perspective."

"It was bad, Lillian. Maybe it wasn't the same kind of bad as other people have gone through, but it's still bad. Being married to someone who only wants to use you is bad. You shouldn't feel guilty for wanting to escape something like that."

"I feel like I'm very lucky because I'm with you."

He smiled. "That's good because it means that getting out of Virginia was the best thing you ever did for me."

She laughed, amused at the way he'd worded that statement. "I don't regret leaving Virginia."

"Good. I never want you to regret coming here." He cupped her face with his hand and brought her mouth to his.

Feeling much better, she relaxed against him and deepened the kiss. He let out a light moan and traced her lower lip with his tongue. She parted her lips for him, inviting him to kiss her more intimately. She'd never get tired of the way he desired her. It was wonderful.

It was much more so now that he knew the truth about her past and still wanted her. Still, she preferred to think of herself as Lillian. Lillian knew how to live in a remote cabin. She knew how to cook and clean. She could milk a cow and tend a garden. Soon, she'd know how to preserve food. Mic had promised to teach her to do that so they'd have plenty of food in the winter. Lillian was a woman who was capable of taking care of herself.

Prudence relied on others to take care of her. She could ride a horse well, and she could play a piano alright. But she couldn't do much else. Attending dinner parties and listening to people ramble on about their interests weren't skills that were useful. They certainly hadn't helped her attain a good husband, nor could they help her out here. Prudence was unloved and lonely. She didn't really have anything.

Prudence was weak. Lillian was strong. Prudence lived with depression. Lillian lived with hope. As far as she was concerned Prudence died the day she left Virginia. Now she was Lillian, and that was who she'd always be.

Mic helped her out of her clothes then hurried to slip his off. He'd become quite skilled when it came to undressing her, but she supposed that was to be expected since he'd done it so often since they married.

He brought her on top of him and continued kissing her, his hands running up and down her back in a way that delighted her. He probably hadn't planned to make love to her tonight.

She hadn't planned for it, either. The bedroll wasn't the most comfortable place to make love, but at the moment, she didn't care about comfort. She wanted to be consumed by his passion, to enjoy everything Lillian had that Prudence never did.

She straddled him until his penis was pressed nicely on her sensitive nub. Already, her body was ready for him. She noted how slick she was as she rubbed herself against him. He let out a moan and cupped her breasts in his hands.

On any other night, she might have taken her time to enjoy being with him, but her body was aching for him and that ache was demanding to be satisfied. She rocked her hips faster. He murmured his encouragement and teased her nipples, an action which further intensified how good she was feeling between her legs.

She bit her lower lip and rubbed up against him in greater urgency, not the least bit shy about voicing her pleasure as she did so. Once more the familiar tension was building up within her, and it demanded to be satisfied. She continued rubbing against him in hopes she might reach the peak this time.

He urged her along, putting his hands on her hips and helping her move faster. She grew closer and closer to the peak, and then suddenly, she was right there. She stilled and cried out. She gripped his arms and rode out the waves of pleasure as they coursed through her.

She had no idea how long she stayed suspended in the heights of bliss, but she savored the moment for as long as she could. When she finally relaxed, she opened her eyes and saw that he was smiling at her.

"You're so beautiful," he whispered. "Now whenever I look at the stars, I'll think back on this moment and remember how radiant you are."

She returned his smile and leaned forward to kiss him. Then, recalling his own need to be satisfied, she took him into her. He let out a contented moan and shifted beneath her so that he could plunge deeper into her. She tightened her hold on his shoulders and began working with him. He felt good. It seemed that after she climaxed, she became more sensitive to him, and right now, his penis was stroking her in just the right places.

This time when she climaxed, he joined her. Her core clenched around him as he filled her with his seed. The waves came softer this time, but she enjoyed it just as much as before. She waited until they both relaxed before she leaned forward and kissed him.

He responded in kind, his tongue interlacing with hers. They spent the next couple of minutes just kissing each other, reluctant to part from this moment in time when it was just the two of them.

Afterward, he brushed her cheek with his thumb and smiled. "You are the most desirable lady around."

She laughed and gave him another kiss. "It's easy to be desirable with you." She settled beside him. "I like how you make me feel. It's nice to know you think I'm attractive."

"Why wouldn't I? It's true."

"You're wonderful, Mic. I can't recall a time I've ever been happier."

"I can't, either."

Smiling, she draped her arm over his waist. It didn't matter that the ground wasn't comfortable like the bed she'd used to sleep in while growing up. It didn't matter that she didn't get to bathe every day. It didn't matter that she couldn't have the cook make anything she wanted. It didn't matter that she wasn't wearing the latest fashion. None of those things mattered because she had much more now than she'd ever had before.

Lillian had the perfect life.

She closed her eyes, and soon, she fell asleep.

Chapter Eleven

Two weeks later, Mic led Lillian down a path about a mile from the cabin. This was part of her training, and while she'd gotten good at being quiet while she walked over leaves and twigs that were strewn across the ground, there were still some things she needed to learn. And today, he was going to teach her something new. He was going to teach her how to hide.

He stopped at a hollow log. The thing had moss all over it, and it was under the shade of a couple of nearby trees. He'd come by the thing over a dozen times since moving out here. That morning while they ate breakfast, he had thought about this log. It just might be her size. He couldn't fit in it, but maybe she could.

"You see that log over there?" he asked, pointing to it.

Her gaze went to it, and she nodded.

"Should you need a place to hide, I think that might be a good one," he said.

"You think I can fit in there?"

"There's only one way to find out."

For a moment, he thought she was going to say no because logs were dirty and full of all kinds of nasty critters, but she took a deep breath and started braiding her hair. "If I'm going to go in there, I don't want to mess up my hair," she explained when he shot her a questioning look.

He chuckled. Only a woman would worry about her hair in a situation like this.

"It's not funny," she replied, amusement in her voice. "It takes a lot of work to clean my hair since it's so long."

"I certainly don't mind you keeping your hair clean, and I don't mind helping you wash it, either." He winked at her.

"From what you said, it won't be too long before it's too cold to go for a swim. I'll have to wash my hair over a pot of hot water. I won't be taking off my clothes to do that."

"You make a good point. Don't braid your hair. It'll give me a good excuse to take you for another swim."

"Is your mind always on lovemaking?"

"No. There's a few minutes in the day when I think about other things."

Laughing, she gave him a playful swat. "You're silly, Mic. But I love it, so don't change."

"I wouldn't dream of it."

She finished braiding her hair. "I'm ready."

He followed her as she quietly made her way over to the log. She tripped over a nearby tree root, so he caught her.

"Good," he told her. "You didn't shriek or anything. If you end up tripping or falling, it's important you don't make a sound."

"But if I fall, won't I make a sound?"

"Yes, but someone might think you're an animal. There are critters all over the place out here."

They reached the log and saw some bugs crawling over it.

She knelt in front of the log and peered into its hollow space. "Something tells me I'm going to be taking that swim after all. I just wasted my time in trying to protect my hair."

"It's a hot day. A swim will be nice."

She frowned. "I was hoping to check some traps and milk the cow. I won't have time to do that if I swim."

"I'll check the traps and milk the cow while you wash up."

"You're not going swimming with me?"

"It doesn't take me long to do those chores. I'll join you before you're done."

With an amused grin, she got on her hands and knees and crawled into the log. She let out a couple of startled shrieks when she came across some bugs, but other than that, she was quiet. Better yet, he saw that she fit in pretty well once she was all the way in. The only thing wrong was that her feet hung out of the end.

"Can you pull your legs up?" he asked.

"I think so," came her muffled reply.

His eyebrows furrowed. "Is your hand over your mouth?"

"Well, I don't want a bug to crawl into it."

He thought about telling her a bug wasn't going to go into her mouth, but there were a couple of times one flew right into his mouth when he was out working, so he refrained from saying anything.

She pulled her feet into the log. He stepped back onto the path and took a good look at the log. He wouldn't know she was in there if he'd just come up to this place. Good. It was an ideal hiding spot.

He returned to the log. "Congratulations. I can't see you at all. You can hide here any time you want."

"Oh joy," she replied, not hiding her sarcasm.

Chuckling, he reached into the log and helped her out. He brushed away the cobwebs and a couple of bugs from her hair and clothes before she became aware of them. "You did great," he said. "I have to hand it to you. You're fitting in fast with this way of life."

She grimaced. "I don't want to hide in logs all the time. I don't mind walking like a ghost through the paths, but finding places to hide aren't my idea of fun."

"They aren't fun. The reason you hide is in case someone is chasing you." Before she had time to dwell on that statement, he put his arm around her shoulders. "I think we did enough for today. Let's head back to the cabin."

The walk back was pleasant, but it seemed that everything he did with her was pleasant. He loved being out here alone with her. It felt as if they were in their own private world. He wanted nothing more than for this peaceful paradise to continue.

Unfortunately, reality reared its ugly head as soon as they arrived at the cabin. Wade, Jeremiah, and Abby had arrived, and that could only mean one thing: it was time to rescue Wade's son.

Wade and Jeremiah were lounging by the barn, talking in quiet tones, while Abby was using a knife to clean the dirt from under her fingernails.

Jeremiah saw Mic and Lillian first. "We were beginning to wonder if something happened to you two," he said as he approached them.

"I was teaching Lillian how to walk quietly and hide," Mic replied.

"Your technique works," Abby said, shoving her knife in the sheath that was hanging on her belt. "I didn't hear you coming." She looked Lillian up and down and smiled. "You fit right in out here. I hardly recognize you. Before, you were wearing that pretty dress. You looked more like a doll than a person. It was no wonder Mic was in such a hurry to marry you. You're one of the prettiest women around."

Lillian's face grew pink with pleasure, but Wade interrupted them before they could exchange any more pleasantries.

"It's time to get my boy," Wade said. "Charles' men left for Denver."

Abby nodded. "I saw them leave a few days ago. They were slow going out, so I gave them an extra day to make sure they weren't coming back for anything."

Mic hid his apprehension. Going up against Charles was no light matter. Yes, they stood a better chance with the majority of his men gone, but he and the others were skilled with a gun.

"How many men stayed behind with Charles?" Mic asked.

"The best I can figure is three," Abby said.

So that made it four against four. He, Wade, Jeremiah, and Abby against Charles and three men. At least that leveled things out on each side.

"When will we go?" Lillian asked.

Mic's eyes grew wide. Did he just hear her ask that in a way that suggested she was going to go with them?

"We should go tonight," Wade said.

"No," Jeremiah argued. "We just got here. We need to stay here for the night and rest. We'll be no good if we're tired."

"Jeremiah's right," Abby said. "We need to be smart about this. The most important thing is that we get your son. We need to be well rested in order to be quick on our feet."

Wade didn't look happy about it but grumbled his agreement.

"This sounds dangerous," Lillian said. "Will we have to take guns with us?"

There it was again. She was acting as if she planned to join them. Mic took her by the arm and pulled her away from the others. While they began to discuss possible strategies for getting Wade's son, Mic whispered, "You will stay here. I don't want to risk you getting hurt."

"I appreciate that, Mic, but what happens if you get hurt?" Lillian whispered in return.

"I'm good with a gun, and I've been trained to be careful when going into dangerous situations. You just got here. I've only had time to teach you how to walk as if you're a ghost. There's much more to learn."

"I realize that, but wouldn't it be better if you had another person helping out?"

"But you're a woman."

"So?" She gestured to Abby. "She's a woman, too."

He blinked. Lillian was right, of course. Abby was a woman. It was just easy to forget that when Abby acted so much like a man. Plus, she knew how to handle herself even in the toughest of situations. She could shoot a target from a long distance, and she never got spooked by anything.

"Abby's different," he said. "She's not your typical woman. She's more like a brother than a sister." He shook his head. "I can't risk it. Wade lost his wife. They weren't in love like you and I are, but it still hurt him when she died. I don't want to lose you."

"I don't have to put myself in harm's way. Can't I at least come along so I'll know whether you're alright or not?" Her eyes lit up. "I can be the lookout. While the four of you go in to get Wade's son, I can watch to see if anyone notices you. I could give out a call or shoot a gun or something to let you know if you're in any danger of getting caught."

"A lookout would come in handy," Wade said.

Mic jerked then spun around to face his brother. He hadn't been aware that Wade had come over to them.

Unapologetic about eavesdropping, Wade continued, "The more people we have, the better. We're not going to get another chance like this for a long time. Let Lillian come along. We'll make sure she's hidden so no one finds her." Without letting Mic respond, he turned to her and asked, "Can you whistle?"

Lillian pursed her lips together and gave out a strong whistle that made Jeremiah and Abby stop talking.

Wade nodded in a way that let Mic know he was pleased by how loud she could whistle. "Can you whistle like this?" Wade asked then whistled, varying the pitch so that he sounded like a bird.

Lillian's eyebrows furrowed for a moment before she tried to imitate him.

"That was close. Try it again. Go higher in the beginning and lower in the middle. Then finish up just as you did a moment ago." He whistled again so she could hear the exact pitches he had used.

She did it again, and this time, she got closer to the mark.

Mic fidgeted as he fought the urge to tell her to stop. He didn't like this. Too many things could go wrong. Lillian was not prepared like the rest of them were, and she was going to be all by herself. He couldn't afford to take her into the house with him because that's where the showdown would take place. But with no one to watch over her, he would be worried about her the entire time when he needed to focus on getting Wade's son.

Lillian whistled a third time, and this one was the perfect imitation of one of the birds in their area. As soon as Mic saw the satisfied smile on the faces of Wade, Jeremiah, and Abby, he knew Lillian would be going with them. She had just proven that she was useful. Mic couldn't claim that she would be a hindrance like he'd originally hoped to.

"Good," Wade said. "We all leave first thing tomorrow morning." Then he returned to Jeremiah and Abby.

Lillian clasped her hands together in excitement. "I've never been of any use to anyone before. For my whole life, it seems that all I've been is a burden."

"You were never a burden to me," Mic replied, hurt she should lump him in with everyone back in Virginia. "You've been useful to me the whole time you've been with me."

Her excitement waned. "I didn't mean that you saw me as a burden. I know you don't see me that way."

"Then you should have appreciated the fact that I was trying to keep you here while the rest of us went to get Wade's son. What good will it do me if you end up dead? If you're caught, that's exactly what will happen to you. Charles isn't going to let you live. The only reason he's letting Wade's son live is because he can turn him against us. Charles is keeping him out of spite. It's his way of letting us know he's in control.

There's no reason for him to keep you alive. We won't have a chance to go in and save you. This isn't something to get excited about."

He could see she was conflicted. Given her past, she desperately wanted to prove she had something of worth to offer those around her that didn't stem from her family's wealth. She wanted to be valued just as she was. But she really hadn't understood she already had that value placed on her simply because she was his wife. She didn't have to prove anything to anyone.

He let out a defeated sigh. "I'll bring in some water so you can wash your hair in the cabin." There was no way he was going to let her wash in the river with Jeremiah and Wade on the property. "We have a lot to do to get ready for tomorrow."

Without another word, he headed for the well.

Chapter Twelve

Lillian sat at the kitchen table in the cabin. She turned her comb over in her hand as she waited for her hair to dry. She still didn't know what to say to Mic. She understood why he was upset. And he was probably right. She'd probably been foolish to be so eager to help him and the others get Wade's son.

It didn't occur to her that she didn't have to do something in order to prove her worth until Mic said, *"You've been useful to me the whole time you've been with me."*

Her parents had lamented the fact that she was a girl. A girl couldn't go out and make more money for the family. Her brother had always been more highly esteemed because he could work for the family business.

There was a knock at the door.

Lillian jumped up and ran to it. She was ready to open it when Abby called out she was the one on the other side. Lillian checked to make sure she had secured all of the buttons on the clean dress she'd put on right after washing her hair. Everything was in place.

She opened the door, and on its own accord, her gaze searched for Mic.

"Mic's helping the others set up for the night," Abby told her as if she had read her mind. "We're all going to sleep out under the stars. This cabin's too small for all of us." Abby gestured to the kitchen. "Mind if I come in?"

"Oh, sorry." Lillian moved aside and let Abby into the cabin. Since the others were busy, she shut the door and followed Abby to the table.

Abby sat down, set her hat aside, and propped her feet up on the table. She pulled the back of her hair up and wiped the back of her neck. Then she wiped her hand on her pants.

"I'll be glad when it gets cooler," Abby said. "I'm not used to all this heat. It's been hotter than usual this summer." Her gaze went to Lillian. "Are you used to a lot of snow?"

Lillian glanced at the table and tried not to think of the traces of mud clinging to the boots. Lillian had been doing her best to keep the cabin clean, and she'd have to wipe the table down after Abby left. Lillian knew Abby wasn't like any of the women in Virginia. None of them would go around hunting rattle snakes or plop their feet on tables. No wonder Mic thought of Abby as a brother rather than a sister.

Forcing her mind off the table, Lillian sat across from her. "There's been snow where I lived."

"I bet it's not like what we get here. Some days the wind will blow it all over the place, and it's impossible to see your hand if you put it right in front of your face." To demonstrate, Abby put her hand a couple feet in front of her. "On those days, you might as well stay in." She put her hand down. "You'll probably be protected by these trees, though. Mic picked a good location here in the mountainside. Not only would Charles never suspect he's out here, but trees are nice to have around when a snow storm hits. Do you have mountains in Virginia?"

"Yes, but I lived by the Atlantic Ocean."

"I've never seen the ocean. What's it like?"

Lillian brought the comb to her hair and started working through the tangles as she considered how to explain what an ocean looked like to someone who'd never seen one. After several long seconds, she said, "I suppose an ocean is like a river that never ends. Or rather, it doesn't seem to end. You look at it, and there's nothing on the other side."

Abby took a moment to think over the explanation and nodded. "I like that. I'll have to tell that to my students when I get back to town."

Lillian had forgotten Abby was a schoolteacher. "The woman I was on the stagecoach with was on her way to Medicine Bow to be a teacher. She mentioned there being a contract that forbids female teachers from marrying."

"She's right. The school board frowns on women getting married while they teach. Unlike men, a woman can get with child, and if that happens, she won't be able to teach her class. She'll need to stay home and take care of the baby. The nice thing about signing the contract to teach is that men leave you alone. They know you can't court or anything."

"Don't you want to get married?"

"Sure, at some point. But right now my biggest worry is getting Lloyd back to Wade. Then I have to help my brothers get the ranch back. After that, I can get married."

Lillian supposed that made sense. With so much going on, it would be hard to focus on being courted.

"Besides," Abby continued, "being a teacher gives me respectability in town, and that allows me to keep a close eye on Charles. I don't have to resort to hiding like Wade and Mic do. Charles doesn't think I can handle a weapon."

Abby lifted one of her pantlegs up, and Lillian saw a knife strapped to her leg. Lillian stiffened. What was Abby planning to do with that thing?

"It's always good to have your secrets," Abby said with a grin. "Men don't think a woman can defend herself. I've always found a knife to be much more effective at hiding than a gun. Plus, no man expects a woman to be carrying one. We can get away with pretending to be helpless. I do that with Charles, and it keeps him from bothering me."

Lillian eyed the knife warily. What was Abby's point in twirling the knife around?

Abby put her feet on the floor, either ignoring the dirt on the table or oblivious to it. She put her elbows on the table and pointed the knife in Lillian's direction. "Do you know how to use one of these?"

It took Lillian a moment to realize Abby was not going to throw the knife at her. She released her breath. "I've cut up fruits and vegetables with them."

"No, that's not what I'm talking about. Do you know how to defend yourself using one of these?"

Lillian shook her head and hurried to comb the rest of her hair. Something told her that Abby was going to teach her how to use a knife whether she was ready for it or not.

And sure enough, Abby said, "Then it's a good thing I came when I did. If you're going to help us, you'll need to be able to defend yourself. We're probably going to be in the house for a while. That will leave you all by yourself."

Forcing aside her unease, Lillian asked, "How long is 'a while'?"

"Not sure. It can be a few minutes to half an hour. There's no telling how messy things will get."

Great. Just what Lillian wanted to hear. She didn't know why she had assumed the task was going to be easy since most of Charles' men would be gone. Now she could appreciate why Mic had advised her to stay here.

But would she really want to be stuck here all by herself, not knowing what was happening to the others? No, no she wouldn't. She'd be frightened to be alone here all by herself. Ever since she was born, she hadn't been alone in a remote area. There had always been someone nearby. And out here, it'd be too easy for someone to hide.

Lillian's attention went back to the knife. "How do you use that thing to defend yourself?"

"I'm glad you're willing to learn. I realize Mic isn't all that thrilled with you joining us, but we could use the help. As long as we're smart about it, everyone will be alright. Using your wits is the most powerful weapon you got. The knife is to be used if you have no other option."

Lillian relaxed. She liked the idea of using her wits more than having to rely on brawn. If Abby was going to approach it from that angle, she just might have a chance of success should she get caught up in the middle of the conflict.

Lillian rose to her feet. "I'll put my comb away then we can get started."

Abby nearly leapt from her chair in unbridled enthusiasm.

Lillian's eyes widened. Was it possible that Abby was looking forward to this confrontation with Charles? She did like to kill rattlesnakes and do other gross things. Maybe facing danger was fun for her.

"I'll wait for you outside." Abby set her hat on her head and hurried out of the cabin.

With a shake of her head, Lillian climbed the ladder to put her comb away.

***

"Wade and Mic, you two will go in through this side," Jeremiah said as he moved the stick in the dirt where he had drawn a crude representation of the ranch. "Abby and I will go in through this side." He moved the stick around the rectangle that represented the house.

"We should put Lillian at the large tree over here." Wade made an X to the north of the property that faced the front of the house. "This is the best location. She'll be able to see everything that's going on from here."

Mic crossed his arms but didn't protest. The others— including Lillian—had agreed that having her there would better their chances. As much as he hated it, they needed every advantage they could get. And did he really have the right to insist she not help when she clearly could? There was a two-year-old boy's life and well-being at stake. Lloyd wasn't just Wade's son; he was Mic's nephew. Mic had a responsibility to rescue the boy. If Lillian was in any kind of trouble, he'd want all the help he could get.

Wade directed their attention to the other diagram they had etched into the dirt. This was of the rooms in the house. "Lloyd's bedroom is here." He put an X in the room. "We'll be going in around midnight, so he'll be asleep."

"That's if Charles didn't move him to another bedroom," Mic said.

"That's always possible," Jeremiah consented. "I'm sure he expects us to come for Lloyd. He probably posted an ad for a mail order bride with the idea of having a woman keep constant watch over him. They all know what kind of man he is. Even the women of ill repute avoid him."

"That doesn't stop him from taking what he wants," Wade muttered, bitterness finding its way into his voice.

"The only way he can get a woman to willingly go to him is to find one who has no idea who he is," Jeremiah said.

Which had made Lillian the perfect target. Mic inwardly shuddered. The others had helped him protect her from marriage to him. He just hoped rescuing Lloyd wasn't going to make the trouble of kidnapping her from the stagecoach of no effect. If Charles or one of his men got their hands on her, he'd never forgive himself for letting her come along.

"As long as we follow the plan, I think we can do this in under thirty minutes," Jeremiah said, drawing their attention back to getting Lloyd. "We have the advantage of knowing the layout of the house."

Yes, that should make rescuing Lloyd easier. Mic felt a little easier about taking Lillian along knowing that.

"Whoever gets Lloyd needs to get out of the house as soon as possible," Wade said. "If we get caught, there's bound to be gunfire, and I don't want to lose him like I lost his mother."

"Whoever gets Lloyd should go to Lillian," Jeremiah replied. "We can leave a horse over at this old shed." He tapped a spot nearby the large tree Lillian would be hiding behind. "Nothing's in there anymore."

Wade nodded in excitement. "That'll work. Whoever gets Lloyd can go with Lillian to this cabin."

Mic felt some of the tension leave his body. At least Lillian's role would be a very small one. The rest of them were far better prepared in case gunfire broke out. And knowing the person who got Lloyd would go to Lillian and then come here was even better.

He heard his sister's laughter coming from near the cabin and turned his gaze to see what had amused her. He saw Abby slapping her leg between fits of laughter. She jabbed the knife in front of her then shook her head in a way that indicated that was not a good way to handle a knife. Lillian, who was standing beside her, looked overwhelmed but determined to listen to what Abby was saying.

"Is there anything else?" Mic asked Wade and Jeremiah.

"No, I think that sums up what we need to do," Jeremiah said. "I'll update Abby on Lillian's part of the plan when she's done teaching Lillian how to adequately use a knife."

"She's always acted more like a boy than a girl," Wade commented with a shake of his head.

"That's coming in handy right now," Jeremiah pointed out. "She's one more person who can help us get Lloyd."

Wade admitted Jeremiah was right and then left to go to the river.

"I'm going to check and make sure we have everything we need for tomorrow night," Jeremiah told Mic then went over to the horses that the others had brought with them.

Mic decided to go over to Abby and Lillian. As he approached, he heard Abby say, "You need to plan what you're going to do with the knife before you use it. The problem with some people is that they are too hasty. It's best to bide your time and wait until the moment is right. Otherwise, you'll end up doing something like this," she swung the knife erratically in front of her, "and while you might cut your rival, you're unlikely to stop them from coming after you."

The two looked over at him, and since neither spoke, he said, "Abby's right. It's best to take your time and think through what you're going to do. You can't let your emotions get in the way. Take a deep breath and calm yourself down. Look at the areas of weakness in your rival. Then strike when that area of weakness is exposed."

Abby nodded. "It's all about using your wits."

Lillian took a deep breath and released it. "Alright. I can do that."

"You'll be on watch at a tree," Mic told her. "It's actually a good spot on the property. No one should see you from there. The rest of us will be in the house to find Lloyd. Whoever gets him will bring him to you, and then you'll go with them back to this cabin." He glanced at Abby. "We're going to do this as quietly and quickly as possible."

"I understand," Abby replied, turning serious. "I know you don't want Lillian to go, but I'm glad she'll be there. Someone ought to be there to alert us if we're spotted."

"We might be spotted inside the house," Mic said. "In that case, it doesn't matter if she's there or not." Before Abby could protest, he hurried to add, "I'm not arguing that she should stay here." He'd already done that to no effect. "I'm just saying that we can't compensate for all possibilities. Anything can happen. We need to be quick to adapt to whatever comes up."

"I know that," Abby replied. "I'm not saying everything will work exactly as we planned. I'm saying that having Lillian with us will give us a better chance of getting our nephew away from Charles. I don't think even he would hurt a two-year-old boy, but the sooner we get Lloyd out of there, the better." She paused then turned back to Lillian. "We should take a break."

Mic silently thanked his sister for allowing him some time alone with Lillian. He could tell by the way Lillian was fiddling with the belt around her waist that she was afraid he was still angry with her. If, God forbid, something bad were to happen tomorrow night, he didn't want there to be any tension between them.

Since the others were lingering around the property, he took Lillian by the hand and led her into the cabin. Once he shut the door, she put her arms around his neck and put her head on his shoulder.

"I'm sorry, Mic," she whispered. "I didn't want to upset you. I was only trying to help."

He shushed her as he rubbed her back. "I know. I'm not mad at you. I'm just worried. You're the best thing that's happened to me, and I don't want to lose you."

"You're the best thing that's happened to me, too. No one really cared about me until you came along."

He wanted to insist that couldn't be true because it would be awful if she had spent a good portion of her life believing she had nothing of value to offer someone, but considering how excited she'd been to be a part of the plan to rescue Lloyd, he knew that it had to be true. For whatever reason, the people in Virginia hadn't valued her. Her worth had been based on her family's wealth, and that had been it.

He let out a heavy sigh and pulled her closer to him. "Try not to think about the past. It doesn't matter. You're with me now, and I love you."

"I love you, too, and I promise to be careful. I'll take everything you and Abby have been teaching me seriously."

He almost wished the whole ordeal was over and Lloyd was already safe with Wade. But he didn't know if that safety would come at the expense of Lillian's life. There were too many things that could go wrong, and as much as he didn't want to think of them, they insisted on cycling through his mind. All he could do was make the most of today. Tomorrow morning, they'd head out to the family ranch. After that, whatever happened was out of his control.

He didn't know how long he spent holding her when a knock came at the door.

"Are you ready to continue with the lesson?" Abby called out.

Lillian chuckled. "I've never come across someone with so much zeal for life."

"Abby takes after our mother," he replied, feeling his mood improving from the simple action of joining Lillian in laughing. "She looks at everything as either a challenge or a reward."

Though reluctant, he opened the door to a young woman who was on a mission to teach Lillian all she could in the short time they had. "Lillian's ready, but I'm going to be with you two."

"Alright." She gestured to a section where there was a break from the shade. "That area will give us the best light. I want to show Lillian some subtle moves she can make should she get caught, and it's easier for her to see what I'm doing if we're directly in the sunlight."

Forcing aside his unease at the possibility of Lillian getting caught by Charles or one of his men, Mic slipped his arm around Lillian's waist, and the two followed Abby to the clearing.

Chapter Thirteen

Around midnight the next night, Lillian was huddled behind a large tree. The others were heading for the yellow two-story house a few hundred feet away from her hiding place. She scanned the property. So far, all was quiet and dark. There was no moving in the house or the bunkhouse.

So far, so good.

She tried not to think about her shaky hands. The whole thing was surreal. This wasn't something she ever would have done back in Virginia. She would have stayed behind at the cabin and kept safe. Maybe she should have done that this time, too. She didn't know Charles, but she got the impression he was as bad as Robert. She recalled the day her brother had introduced her to Robert. The feeling of dread in the pit of her stomach matched the feeling she experienced right now.

She didn't want to think of the dangerous mission they were on. She needed to focus on the two-year-old child in that house. The most important thing was to get him out of there.

A coyote howled in the distance, and she involuntarily shivered. Her hand went to the knife hidden under her skirt. It was still secure in the leather strap wrapped around her calf. She recalled what Abby had told her about handling a knife if something came at her. Of course, Abby had been talking about a person, but the maneuver should work on an animal, should one attack. She gave a quick glance around her. The only animal nearby was the horse waiting for Lloyd.

She released her breath and turned her attention back to the house. She must not think of the animals lurking around the place. She must concentrate on alerting the others in case someone had caught them.

She watched as Mic and Wade made their way around one side of the house. Abby and Jeremiah went around the opposite side. Her vantage point gave her a better view of Abby and Jeremiah. She watched as Jeremiah opened a window.

Lillian glanced at the bunkhouse. All was dark in there. Her gaze went back to Abby and Jeremiah. He gave Abby a boost to help her in, and then he followed her in.

Lillian scanned the house. She didn't see any candles or kerosene lamps flicker with light. That was good. No one was aware people were going into the house.

The coyote howled again, but this time, the sound was further away. That made her feel a little better. She dug her fingers into the bark of the tree as her gaze swept across the property. She didn't see anything. By now, Mic, Wade, Jeremiah, and Abby were in the house.

Soon it would be over. They would get Lloyd and bring him out. Then they would all be safe and together at Mic's cabin.

The horse nearby neighed. She glanced over her shoulder. The steed looked agitated. She frowned and directed her attention back to the house and bunkhouse. What had the steed noticed? What was she missing?

And then she saw a light come on in the bunkhouse. She gasped and then whistled to let the others know there was movement on the property.

The light went out in the bunkhouse. Lillian's fingers dug further into the tree bark. The man in the bunkhouse knew. He wasn't fooled by the whistle. He knew it'd been a signal. And since he had put the light out, they were at a disadvantage. She didn't know if she should whistle again or not. If the man in the bunkhouse had heard her, then it was likely Mic, Wade, Jeremiah, and Abby had heard her, too.

She watched the bunkhouse for any signs someone was going to make their way to the house. She heard a gunshot. Startled, her gaze went back to the house. It'd come from one of the rooms in there. And then she saw a couple of men running from the bunkhouse to the house.

Without thinking, she whistled again. She winced. What a stupid move. Mic, Wade, Jeremiah, and Abby were already aware someone had noticed them.

I need to calm down. I need to think clearly. Watching as the men made their way into the house, she forced herself to take a couple of deep breaths and slowly release them. She had to keep her wits about her.

More gunfire erupted from within the house, and she had no way of figuring out the exact location it was coming from. For all she knew, it was coming from different rooms.

A trickle of sweat made its way down her forehead, but she kept her focus on the house. A light came on in one of the rooms, along with another gunshot.

Her stomach clenched in dread. This couldn't be good. Someone had to be wounded. There had been too many gunshots for her to conclude otherwise.

As another gunshot rang through the air, she saw someone running out of the house. The person was heading in her direction. She squinted. It looked as if the person was holding a young child.

Did they do it? Did they manage to get Lloyd?

More gunfire erupted from within the walls of the house. Her gaze darted to it, but she didn't see anyone else coming out of it. The only person who'd made it out was the person running right for her. It had to be Mic, Wade, Jeremiah, or Abby. They were the only ones who knew the horse was waiting here with her.

She studied the person racing toward her and realized it was Abby. Lillian hurried to get the horse. She would have to worry about the others later. Right now, she had to focus on getting them back to Mic's cabin. She hurried to the abandoned shed. As she made her way around the dark corner, she bumped into someone's hard chest. She shrieked and tried to step back, but the man grabbed her by the arm to stop her.

She'd been caught. Despite their best efforts, someone had noticed her and had been hiding here with the getaway horse.

Abby ran behind the shed with Lloyd in her arms. "Lillian, are you alright?" she whispered.

"Oh, she's just fine," her captor replied.

The hairs on the back of her neck stood on end. She'd know that voice anywhere. It was Robert.

He moved from the shadows, dragging her with him. He looked her up and down and clucked his tongue. "You've been a very bad girl. The detective said you had come out to be with Charles Gray, but I didn't really believe it until I saw it for myself."

"Lillian, what's going on?" Abby asked as she shifted the sleepy boy in her arms.

Robert's eyebrows rose. "Going by your middle name? Why not tell everyone who you really are, Prudence Van Horn?"

Lillian glanced between Robert and Abby. She could tell Abby was preparing for a fight in order to help her, but Lillian couldn't let her do that when she had an innocent child in her arms.

She needed to come up with something in order to gain an advantage in this situation. Robert had her exactly where he wanted her. If she didn't say and do the right thing, she would put herself and the others in more trouble than they were already in.

After taking a moment to think through all of her options, she burst into tears and clung to Robert. "Thank God you're here. I made a terrible mistake in leaving Virginia."

Robert's eyebrows furrowed, and he glanced at Abby.

"Outlaws kidnapped me from the stagecoach," Lillian continued. "They made me stay with them. They threatened all kinds of horrible things if I didn't do what they wanted." She wrapped her arms around his neck and turned him so that he wasn't looking at Abby. "Please get me out of here. I'm scared." She motioned for Abby to take the horse and leave.

Abby winced.

Lillian motioned for her to take Lloyd out of there again then stepped back and looked at Robert, hoping he would keep his attention on her. "The idea of marriage just put me into a panic, and I...I..."

"You did a very stupid thing," he finished for her.

"Yes, I did. Oh Robert, I was so wrong. Can you ever forgive me?" she asked as more tears filled her eyes.

He groaned. "For heaven's sakes. Get a hold of yourself, Prudence. I can't take the crying anymore." He picked a handkerchief from his pocket and gave it to her.

Lillian saw Abby get on the horse with Lloyd. Abby gave her another uncertain look, and Lillian used the handkerchief to wave for her to go before she dabbed her eyes.

"I'm sorry," Lillian said. "I'll try to stop crying. It's just that they were so scary. You wouldn't believe how uncivilized they are."

Abby gave the horse a soft kick in the sides, and the steed trotted quietly away.

"It was terrible, Robert," she continued so that he would keep his attention on her. "They eat insects and snakes. They sleep outside on the ground. They bathe outdoors." She shivered and wiggled into his arms. "And you wouldn't believe the other things they do."

"That's what you get for running off," he snapped. "You acted like a petulant child. You ran out here to be a mail-order bride."

Oh. That part didn't work in her favor. "A mail-order bride? I didn't come out here to be a bride. I came out here to be a governess to a little boy. That's the ad I answered. Mr. Gray said he was bringing out another lady to marry. He said she was used to the finer things in life and that she didn't know the first thing about being a mother. I thought I was coming out here to help her." She wiped another tear away. "I'm so confused."

He groaned. "You're as stupid and useless as ever. Very well. I'm here now, and I'll clear up this mess. I need to explain things to Charles because he said you thought you were going to marry him."

She clasped her hands together and squeezed them as tightly as she could to ward off the urge to run away. He was going to take her into the house? He was going to take her to Charles? What if Charles showed him the letter she'd written to him? In that letter, it was obvious she expected to marry Charles. If Robert read that letter, he'd know she was lying. And if he knew that, then he'd... She couldn't think of it. She didn't want to think about what he'd do if he knew she was lying.

"Let's get this over with," Robert muttered as he took her by the arm and led her to the house.

There were a couple of rooms lit in the house now, and there was some yelling. She thought she heard a man telling others to search the house and other buildings on the property, but she didn't hear any gunshots. She didn't know if that was a good sign or not.

She prayed that Mic, Wade, and Jeremiah had gotten out of the house. She hoped they were alright. She hoped they would all go to Mic's cabin. And, most of all, she hoped she would figure out a way to escape from Robert so she could get back to Mic where she belonged.

***

120

"Here's the price for Prudence," Robert told Charles as he threw a roll of bills on Charles Gray's desk. Robert glanced at Lillian. "I have to pay for the price on your head, my dear. Were you aware that your association with the outlaws made you one, too?"

Lillian shook her head and lowered her gaze because she had to play the part of a contrite young lady who'd learned that she better let Robert tell her what to do. She took a deep breath and forced her body to remain still.

What she really wanted to do was search the house to see if she could find Mic, Wade, or Jeremiah. That was impossible, of course. Robert wasn't going to let her out of his sight. At least not right now. She'd have to bide her time until it was safe to escape to get away from him.

Men rushed about the house, and she thought she heard one of Charles' men shouting, "Get him!"

She dug her fingernails into the palms of her hands. Which *him* were they talking about? Who, specifically, were they hunting? Mic, Wade, or Jeremiah?

"Five hundred dollars, Prudence," Robert called out to her.

She turned her attention to him.

Robert snickered at her. "He thinks you're worth five hundred."

She forced her face to remain expressionless. Why wouldn't Robert think that amusing? He knew full well she was worth way more than that. But there was no sense in letting Charles know that. She didn't need to start a bidding war over her. Charles was just as terrible as Robert. If she had come here off the stagecoach, she would have recognized the lust for greed in Charles' eyes as soon as she saw him.

She'd seen that her entire life. Her father had it. Her brother had it. Robert had it. And Charles had it, too. She would have tried to run off, but she doubted she would have been able to get away from him since even with most of his men gone, there was no denying how ruthless they were from all the swearing that was going on in the other rooms.

Charles' eyes met hers.

With a shudder, she hurried to look away. He was a good-looking man. He resembled Mic and Wade, except that his skin was lighter, and he had a stockier frame.

"So," Robert directed his gaze at Charles, "where's her trunk?"

Charles shrugged as he tucked the bills into his pocket. "Who cares? You got the girl. That's what you said you wanted. I drew the outlaws here by letting over half of my men leave for Denver. I told you they wouldn't be able to resist coming here for that kid, and they would bring her with them to keep lookout since they needed the help."

Lillian gritted her teeth. This had been a setup. All along, Charles had been expecting them. They hadn't taken him by surprise at all.

"The girl comes with the trunk," Robert told Charles. One of my acquaintances saw her take it on the train with her."

Lillian winced. Robert had been keeping tabs on her after they were engaged?

Charles rolled his eyes as he went to the decanter close by the desk. "It's not my fault that you didn't keep track of the girl or her trunk."

Robert frowned. "I'm not amused. She came here with that trunk. Where is it?"

Charles turned from the decanter and glared at him. "How would I know? When the stagecoach got here, she and the trunk were gone. The outlaws probably insisted she take it so she'd have something to wear." He gestured to Lillian. "That outfit she's got on is fancier than anything they could give her."

As Charles poured himself a drink, Robert glanced her way. She opted to avert her gaze. She wouldn't, under any circumstance, let him know where the trunk was. No matter what happened to her, he was not going to get his greedy hands on it. The money could be used by Mic and his family.

Robert turned his attention back to Charles. "If I find out you have the trunk, I'll have you gutted like a fish."

Charles snorted as he set the lid back on the decanter. "I'd like to see you try." Charles took a sip of his brandy and sneered at him. "You have no idea who you're messing with."

A tense moment passed before Robert let out a frustrated huff and walked over to Lillian. She stiffened but didn't bolt for the door. Robert knelt in front of her, and since he expected her to look at him, she did.

"Prudence, my dear, I want you to think carefully," he said in a calm tone. "You took a trunk with you when you came out to this territory. You remember that trunk, don't you?"

She bit her tongue so she wouldn't snap that she wasn't stupid. She hated it when people spoke to her that way. She'd always hated it, but she didn't realize how much she hated it until Mic treated her like she could think for herself. But since she couldn't afford to give up the plan she'd created to keep Robert from Mic and his family, she needed to play along.

"Yes, I remember," she said. "I needed something to put my clothes in."

He smiled. "Good. Now we're getting somewhere. What happened to that trunk?"

She shrugged. "I don't know."

His smile waned. "What do you mean you don't know? You took it with you when you left Virginia. It had to have been with you on the stagecoach when you came out here."

"It was on the stagecoach. The scary outlaws took it when they took me to their secret hideout. I'm not sure what they did with it."

"How could you not know what they did with it?"

"I had to ride on a horse with one of them, and the thing was behind me. I didn't see what happened to it."

Robert rolled his eyes, but it was Charles who shook his head and muttered, "Women."

Robert sighed then asked her, "Do you know where the scary outlaws' secret hideout is?"

She noted the way Charles' eyebrows rose in interest and gulped. He had to draw them out to him tonight because he didn't know where Mic and the others were hiding. She was sure he'd love for her to reveal where Mic's cabin was, but she would die before that happened.

She directed her gaze to Robert, leaned toward him, and whispered, "Can we leave? That man over there frightens me."

It wasn't a complete lie. There was something cold in his eyes that made her wary of him. It was no wonder Mic didn't want her to go with them to rescue Lloyd. And hadn't his instincts been right? Charles had set a trap for them, and they'd fallen right into it because Robert had offered Charles $500 for her.

"Sure, we can, Prudence." Robert took her by the arm and helped her up. He looked over at Charles. "I have nothing else I need from you."

Charles looked amused. "I'm the one who decides if I have a use for something or not." His gaze went to Lillian. "I don't expect you to see those outlaws again, but in case you do, let them know I allowed them to get Lloyd back. I could have kept him longer if I wanted to. They'll never get the advantage over me, no matter how hard they try." He poured himself another glass of brandy then waved for Robert to take her out.

Robert escorted her out of the room and down the hall. She heard something shatter in the other room and a round of gunshots. On instinct, she let out a shriek and ducked.

Robert grabbed her arm and pulled her up. "They're not shooting in the hall. You're alright."

She didn't know if a bullet could make its way through the wall. Robert obviously didn't think so. But she didn't know for sure, and that uncertainty was worth being careful. If nothing else, he should want to keep her alive just because he wanted to get his hands on her money. She wasn't worth anything to him as long as he didn't have that trunk.

She wasn't stupid. As soon as he got the trunk, he was going to get rid of her. She didn't know if he'd kill her, leave her to the wolves, or something else, but she was determined that no matter what happened, he wasn't going to find that trunk. She'd come too far to back out of this now. She was going to see it through to the end.

They made it onto the porch, and a few feet from them, someone came crashing through one of the windows. Lillian gasped, freed herself from Robert, and hurried down the porch steps.

Robert caught up to her and pulled her back to him. "Where do you think you're going?"

"Are you so daft that you can't tell? I'm getting away from all the gunshots and people who are being thrown out of windows!" she snapped.

The words came without thinking. She'd been so terrified that she hadn't even considered what the ramifications of them might be. And the slap he sent across her cheek let her know that he wouldn't tolerate her snapping at him again.

"You will never call me daft again," he hissed. "I was smart enough to track you down, wasn't I? I know you took your money with you in that trunk. You shouldn't underestimate me, Prudence!" He yanked on her arm and practically threw her at the horse he had waiting for them.

She stumbled into it.

"Well, well, well," a familiar voice called out. "Robert managed to find you after all."

She turned her attention to the two men who were approaching them on their horses. She cringed. Wilson and Daniel. Two of Robert's so-called acquaintances. Her brother had once told her they did Robert's dirty work. Now she knew how true that really was.

"Get on the horse, Prudence," Robert said, his tone sharp.

She hurried to comply. She'd already upset Robert, and that put her in a precarious position. He wasn't likely to be as gentle with her as he had been unless she did exactly what he wanted. He got into the saddle behind her. She grimaced, trying not to notice the way his body felt against hers.

"She and the outlaws came from that way," Daniel told Robert, pointing toward the mountain range that led to Mic's cabin.

"Then that's the way we'll go," Robert said.

Out of the corner of her eye, Lillian saw someone come out on the porch. It was a woman. Surprised, Lillian studied the woman as she knelt over the man—Wade!—who'd been thrown through the window.

Her jaw dropped. It couldn't be!

But it is!

It was Millie!

But how did she end up with Charles? She was supposed to be a teacher in Medicine Bow.

Millie helped Wade to his feet. Wade wavered, and Lillian saw something red covering his clothes. Blood. He'd been injured.

Robert snapped the reins, and the four headed off the land before Lillian could see what happened to Wade and Millie. She didn't hear any more gunshots. She assumed that meant Charles had told his men to stop shooting. He had led them into a trap this evening. He'd said that he had let Lloyd get away. Was it possible he was letting Wade get away, too? Was he hoping Wade would die from his injury? Was he playing cat and mouse with Mic, Wade, Jeremiah, and Abby? Was this all a game to him?

The horse leapt over a rock, and Lillian almost lost her balance. Robert put his arm around her waist and pulled her tightly against him. She gagged. She should have been holding onto the saddle horn instead of worrying about what Charles' motives were for letting Wade, Abby, and Lloyd go. All she could do was hope that he'd let Mic and Jeremiah go, too, and maybe, when all was said and done, she'd find her way back to Mic.

Chapter Fourteen

The sun was high up in the sky when Robert ordered Daniel and Wilson to stop. They had made it to the tree-lined path where she, Mic, Wade, Abby, and Jeremiah had been the day before. That meant Mic's cabin was a day's journey away.

"We'll take a break here," Robert said.

Daniel and Wilson breathed an audible sigh of relief as they got off their horses. In his impatience to get to her trunk, Robert had only allowed them one break. Lillian was just as glad for the break as the others. Not only was she tired, but her body was sore from leaning forward as far as possible to avoid touching Robert any more than she had to while on the horse. Once she was down from the steed, she stretched her muscles in an attempt to feel better.

Daniel and Wilson went to a nearby stream with their canteens. She'd wait until they were gone before going over there to drink and wash her face.

"Alright," Robert told her as he removed the hat from his head and wiped the sweat from his brow. "We saw you with those scary outlaws on this trail, so we know they live somewhere around here." He pointed to a break in the path that went further up the trail. One went to the right and one went to the left. "Which of those will lead us to their hideout?"

"The one on the left," she replied, intentionally choosing the one that would take them away from Mic's cabin.

He frowned at her. "Are you sure? You answered that question a little too quickly."

"When they brought me up here, I was tracking the path in case I could escape and needed to notify the marshal about where the outlaws were hiding. I used little tricks to remember the correct way to go. When I came to the fork in this path, I wondered why I left Virginia. Left is the way to go to get to their hideout."

He narrowed his eyes at her. "That's surprisingly smart for someone who doesn't possess much intelligence."

It was on the tip of her tongue to ask him why he was depending on her to lead him to her trunk when he thought she was stupid, but she managed to hold the retort back. Instead, she settled for shrugging in a way that indicated she didn't know why she'd come up with the trick. The fact that he thought her to be stupid was working to her advantage. It was allowing her time to figure out a way to escape.

"I'm going to go further away from the group," Daniel called out. "I have to take care of something more personal."

Lillian was sure he worded things that way for her sake. Even out in this rugged territory, she was still a lady. She knew very little about Daniel and Wilson, but they seemed to be more gentlemanly than Robert or Charles.

"You got five minutes," Robert replied.

"Five minutes?" Wilson asked. "When are we supposed to eat? The last time I had anything was last night at dinner."

"If you'd eat now instead of talking, you won't have to be hungry when you get back on the horse," Robert said.

Wilson rolled his eyes and trudged over to the horse. He flipped the leather sack open and retrieved a piece of jerky from it.

"If you got to do anything, you should do it now," Robert told her as he set the hat back on his head. "I don't intend to make many stops. But, don't go too far." His lifted his suit jacket and showed her the gun he'd been hiding. "Understand?"

Daniel and Wilson had guns, too. It'd been the only reason she hadn't pulled the knife from under her skirt and used it while she was on the horse with Robert. Knowing Robert also had a gun put her at a further disadvantage. Her best recourse was to slip away like a ghost, but she didn't know how she was going to do that when they were all in close proximity. Sure, there were lots of trees around them, but he was keeping track of her. She couldn't just slip away without him noticing.

Resigned for staying the course for the time being, she nodded to Robert and then hid behind a bush to relieve her bladder.

After she washed her face and drank water at the stream, everyone but Daniel was ready to go. Wilson had a couple sticks of jerky in his hand and was already on the horse. Robert was pacing back and forth in front of his horse. Daniel's horse was tied to a tree. It neighed, as if to notify them that it was impatient to leave.

Robert waited for another minute before he pulled out his pocket watch. "What's taking him so long? We've been here for seven minutes already."

"I warned him not to have those beans," Wilson said. "Those never do him any favors."

Not looking the least bit amused, Robert cupped his hands around his mouth and yelled, "Daniel, it's time to go! Finish things up!"

They waited for another minute, and still, Daniel wasn't anywhere.

Robert grunted as he tucked his pocket watch into his pocket. "Go find him and bring him back," he told Wilson.

Wilson shook his head. "I'm not going to interrupt a man when he's answering nature's call."

Robert glowered at him. "I'm paying you to do what I want. Now go get him."

Wilson groaned but got off his horse. Mumbling something under his breath about not getting paid enough for watching another man empty his bowels, he headed down the path that Daniel had taken.

Lillian bit her lower lip. Should she use the knife now? Robert wasn't looking at her. He was rubbing his eyes. She glanced at Wilson. He was a good distance away, and he had his back to them. Her gaze went back to Robert. Maybe if she acted fast, she could make it work.

She bent down and touched the hem of her skirt. Just as she pulled the skirt up to her calf, Robert lowered his hands and looked in her direction. She paused. Did he see the knife? Her fingertips were at the base of the cool blade.

"For goodness' sakes, put your skirt down," Robert snapped at her. "I'm not interested."

Her jaw dropped. Oh, he couldn't be serious. He didn't honestly think she wanted to…to… Just thinking about it made her gag. Having been with Mic, she knew what Robert was thinking, and there was no way she could ever let him touch her that way. She couldn't believe how arrogant Robert was. Despite what he thought, none of the ladies she'd talked to were attracted to him, and she certainly didn't want to share a bed with him. It'd been one of the reasons she'd bolted out of Virginia.

"I'm scratching an itch," she told him, forcing her tone to remain pleasant. She lowered the skirt and straightened up. "A bug bit me while I was on the horse."

He gave her a look that let her know he didn't believe her.

"You made me straddle the horse like a man," she insisted. "That left my ankles exposed."

Thankfully, the skirt was long enough to cover the top of her calf where the knife was hidden, or she'd really be in trouble right now. She'd hate to be stranded out here without anything to protect herself.

"I can't find him," Wilson called out.

Turning her attention to Wilson, she watched as he wound around the trees to get back to them.

"What do you mean you can't find him?" Robert asked.

"I mean exactly what I said," Wilson replied. "He's nowhere."

"You weren't gone for long. Go search again."

"I found the spot he used nature for an outhouse," Wilson said. "I'm not going any further than that."

"Well, where did he go?"

"How would I know? I wasn't with him when he decided to take off."

Robert looked incredulous. "Why would he leave? He doesn't get paid until I get her trunk." He pointed to Lillian.

"Maybe he doesn't want to do this anymore," Wilson replied. "Maybe he saw how rude you're being to Miss Van Horn and decided he didn't want to be a part of it."

"Rude? You call how I'm acting 'rude'?"

"Well, you did slap her for running away from a brawl and have been making comments about how stupid she is."

"She is to be my wife. I can treat her however I want."

Wilson shook his head but didn't say anything as he got on his horse.

Robert marched over to the trail Daniel had taken and yelled for Daniel to get back to the group. A minute of uncomfortable silence passed with Robert calling out to Daniel a couple more times.

"I just thought of something," Wilson said after Robert called out to Daniel a fourth time. "What if a bear got him?"

"We would have heard a bear if it attacked," Robert replied.

"Alright, then what about snakes?" Wilson asked. "I heard there are rattlers out in this area. They like to hide in bushes, and there are plenty of those around here."

Or maybe Mic or Jeremiah got to him. Lillian blinked in surprise as soon as the thought came to her. She scanned their surroundings. All she saw were trees and bushes. To her, there were no hiding places. But for someone like Mic or Jeremiah, this area might have a lot of them.

She turned her attention to the path leading to the secluded spot Daniel had picked. With the rest of them distracted, it would be easy for someone like Mic to get to Daniel. She didn't know if Jeremiah had the same skill of being quiet as he walked through the wooded area. She hadn't seen anyone follow them to the trees, but then, she hadn't been looking back. She hadn't been able to do that with Robert right behind her. Had any of the men looked back? Or maybe Mic or Jeremiah knew an alternate way to get to this path and had taken that instead of following them directly.

She glanced at Robert and Wilson. Neither seemed to suspect they'd been followed.

Robert went to Daniel's horse. "Prudence, you'll be taking this horse."

Wilson frowned. "What if something serious happened to him? Maybe he's not answering because he can't."

"If something happened to him, or if he decided he didn't want to be a part of this, then that's his problem." Robert brought the horse to Lillian and gave her the reins. He pulled out his gun. "You'll be leading the way. If you stray off the path, I'll put a bullet in your right arm. Then you won't be able to write another letter to a man who's looking for a mail-order bride or a governess."

"Is it really necessary to threaten her?" Wilson asked.

"She came with four outlaws," Robert said, keeping his hard gaze on her. "I only saw two leave that house."

She resisted the urge to show her disappointment. So he'd figured it out. Wilson might not have connected the dots, but he had. And now he was on the alert for Mic or Jeremiah.

He waved the gun toward the saddle on the horse. "Get on."

She did as he wished and made sure her skirt wasn't showing the knife strapped to her leg. If she had to guess, Mic or Jeremiah was alone. If they were together, they would have shown themselves once Daniel was out of the way. As it was, a single person was still outnumbered since Robert and Wilson were still with her.

While Robert went to his horse, she searched the area. Again, she didn't see anyone. There wasn't even a horse. Mic or Jeremiah had to have taken a horse to the place where the trees began because Robert, Daniel, and Wilson had been riding fast until then. Once they reached the trees, they slowed significantly.

"Alright," Robert called out once he was on the horse. "Prudence, lead the way. I'll follow. Wilson, you'll be last."

Her gaze went to the gun Robert had pointed at her. Somehow, knowing that Mic or Jeremiah was nearby made her even more nervous. Robert was now alert to everything around them, and that put Mic or Jeremiah at a disadvantage. With a shaky breath, she urged the horse forward and went to the left path.

***

Mic waited until the horses left the small clearing by the stream before he wiggled out of the hollow log. The space had been tight, but he'd managed to squeeze in after removing his weapons, boots, and hat. Once he was out of the log, he checked the route Lillian was taking Robert and Wilson. Smart girl. She was leading them away from the cabin.

He hurried to put his boots on. Then he put the gun back in the holster at his side and slid the knife into the sheath next to the gun. He picked up the rolled-up rope and put it over his shoulder.

He went to a tree not far from him where he had tied Daniel up. Daniel saw him and tried to scream, but the bandana Mic had tied around his mouth kept him quiet. Mic checked the knot to make sure Daniel was secure. Good. Daniel wasn't going anywhere.

"Since you didn't hurt my wife, I'll let you live," Mic whispered to him once Daniel stopped trying to scream. "It's going to be a while, but I'll make sure you get to the marshal."

He turned from Daniel and hurried up the side of the mountain where Lillian was leading the others.

Chapter Fifteen

"We've been by here before," Robert called out. "Stop!"

Lillian pulled the reins back on her horse and turned the steed around so she could face him. He was glowering at her.

"I recognize that tree," Robert told her. "It has branches that are twining around one another toward the stream."

She had hoped Robert hadn't caught onto the fact that she'd been guiding them in zigzags that ended up going into a huge loop.

She scanned the area, certain Mic or Jeremiah was still following. But she still couldn't see either one of them. She'd been waiting for Robert to suggest they take a break in hopes that Mic or Jeremiah would find a way to detain Wilson. Robert would never let her out of his sight, but Wilson didn't have a reason to keep a close eye on her.

"There are so many trees," she finally said. "It's hard to know where we're going. I'll think better if we take a break."

"I agree with her," Wilson said. "It's hot. We're tired. We're hungry. And I've been having trouble keeping track of where we've been."

Robert glanced over his shoulder and barked, "Who's in charge here?"

"You are," Wilson replied, "but we need to rest and eat."

"That's exactly what she'd like us to do." Robert directed his gaze back to her. "Then your outlaw can get to me or Wilson the way he got to Daniel."

She wasn't sure what to say to that, so she opted to keep quiet.

"We keep going," Robert said. "No one gets off their horse."

Wilson groaned. "I'm exhausted. Can't we find a place that will serve as a barrier between us and the outlaw who's tracking us?"

"And why would I do that?" Robert asked. "So we can jump back on the horses and play this game of diversion again?" Robert directed his gun to Lillian. "I've grown weary of the game, Prudence. It ends now. From this point forward, you are going to take us to your trunk."

"She's not playing a game with us, Robert. She's just tired."

"Don't be an imbecile. She's misdirecting us on purpose. She's sided with the outlaws. She's protecting them." He glared back at her. "I guess you enjoy being passed around the campfire like a whore."

"That's enough!" Wilson yelled. "She's a lady. Watch how you're talking."

"What?" Robert's head whipped back in his direction. "Do you honestly think she's still a virgin after being kidnapped by a group of outlaws? They're all a bunch of uncivilized savages."

"I'm surprised you think my money's still intact since you assume my virginity isn't," Lillian snapped, her anger getting the best of her.

How dare he insinuate Mic and the others had treated her so poorly? Until they came along, no one had treated her well. For all the claim of a civilized culture she was raised in, the people around her had treated her as no better than an object. And what was Robert doing now? All he wanted was her money. She had no use to him otherwise.

Noting the look of shock on Robert's face, she spat, "You think a nice suit, a fancy home, and schooling makes you civilized? The only person you care about is yourself. I might not care for my brother, but you swindled him out of his money and then you threatened to ruin his reputation if he didn't figure out a way to give you more money. You're the uncivilized savage."

Robert's expression turned dark. He pointed his gun at her arm and cocked it. She closed her eyes and braced for the pain. She heard a gunshot. Then another one. But she didn't feel anything. It wasn't until she realized Robert had cried out that she opened her eyes. He fell off the horse and landed on the ground. His horse neighed and ran toward her. Her own horse bucked back. She renewed her grip on the reins and managed to stay in the saddle.

"Who's there?" Wilson called out as he swung his gun around and searched for the person who'd shot Robert.

She didn't know if Wilson was going to panic and shoot his gun, but she decided not to take her chances. She hurried to get off her horse and darted for the nearest tree. She lifted the edge of her skirt and pulled out the knife.

"Don't let her get away!" Robert told Wilson as he struggled to get up.

"But someone out there is shooting at us," Wilson said, his arm still swinging the gun precariously around.

Robert managed to get to his feet, clasping his bloody hand with his good one. He swore and pulled out a handkerchief to help soak up the blood.

After a tense moment of silence, Robert called out, "You can have her. I don't want her. All I want is her trunk. Give me the trunk and you can have her back."

There was no response.

Lillian once again searched for Mic or Jeremiah, but it was impossible to make anything out with all the trees and bushes that surrounded the main path.

Robert let out a heavy sigh. "Fine." He motioned to Wilson. "Get Prudence. If they don't want her, they won't get her."

Lillian didn't think it possible, but Wilson's face went even whiter. "Let her go," he told Robert. "We'll find the trunk another way."

Robert gritted his teeth. "If they get her, they'll take the trunk. Then we won't get anything. You do want to get paid, don't you?"

Wilson's head darted around the area. "They could be closing in on us. Look at your hand. They're not messing around."

"And neither are we," Robert replied.

Robert glanced Lillian's way. With a gasp, she scooted further around the trunk of the tree. She clutched the knife. Focus. She had to focus. The worst thing she could do was panic.

"Wilson, get her," Robert snapped. "She's right over there."

She winced. Just as she feared. Robert had seen her. She glanced at the other trees, but there wasn't one close enough to get to without being caught. Her best recourse was to rely on her wits. Right now, things were equal. She and Mic or Jeremiah were hiding in the trees while Robert and Wilson were on the path. She renewed her grip on the knife.

She peeked around the side of the tree and saw that Robert had let go of his wounded hand. He was bending down. After a moment, she realized he was getting his gun.

"What are you waiting for, Wilson?" Robert asked.

"As soon as I get down from the horse, they're going to shoot me," Wilson said. "I'm not getting her. If you want her, you'll have to get her yourself."

Robert aimed his gun at Wilson. "They may or may not shoot you. On the other hand, I will unless you get her."

Wilson gave one more glance at the area then got down from his horse. He tied the reins to a nearby tree.

"Hurry up," Robert snapped. "We don't have all day." He turned his attention back to her.

She didn't know if he could see her or not, but she refused to look away. She had to know what he and Wilson were doing. She needed to keep her focus on what was going on.

Wilson went around the horse, scanned the area, and then slowly made his way toward her. She took a deep breath and slowly released it. She could do this. It was just a matter of concentrating. She had the element of surprise on her side. As soon as he came within striking distance, she would step out from behind the tree and make her move.

But Wilson didn't get that close. By the time he was a few feet from her, a bullet hit the arm holding the gun. He screamed and dropped the gun.

Robert directed his gun in the direction the shot had come from and fired his own gun. Mic or Jeremiah shot his gun at Robert, but Robert was running for a nearby tree. More gunfire erupted as the men took shots at each other.

Wilson stumbled back and tripped over a large tree branch. He looked over at Robert, shook his head, and hurried off into the trees that would take him far from the gunfight.

Lillian followed the direction Robert was pointing his gun, and after waiting for Mic or Jeremiah to fire his gun, she found the hiding spot. She saw Mic kneeling behind a large tree trunk. Just as she suspected only one person had been following them.

Which meant she had an advantage. Mic was a good shot, but even he wouldn't be able to stop Robert since Robert wasn't in plain view. She was going to have to help him.

She huddled low. Making sure Robert wasn't looking her way, she went to a tree that was closer to him. Her heart beat fiercely in her chest. She could do this. Just focus. Concentrate. She went to another tree. And then another.

The gunshots came to an abrupt stop just as she stepped on a branch. The branch snapped, and Robert glanced her way. She dodged behind the nearest tree, but it was too late. He'd seen her.

Her gaze went to where Mic was hiding, and she saw that he was putting more bullets in his gun. Then she saw that Robert was running straight for her. He aimed the gun at her. With a gasp, she hid back behind the tree. There was no gunshot. She peered around the other side of the tree.

Swearing, Robert threw the gun down and continued heading for her. Mic shot at him, but he darted behind a tree.

What should she do? Stay there and wait, or try to run?

No. She couldn't outrun him. He was stronger than her. All she could do was outwit him. She slipped her arm behind her back so he couldn't see the knife she was holding.

Robert was able to dodge another bullet as he went from one tree to another. She glanced in Mic's direction. He was now running toward her, but Robert would reach her first.

She made sure the knife was pointing away from her then tightened her hold on it. If he got to her, she would have to act fast. She'd probably only get one chance to stab him.

Robert was two trees away from her. He bolted from one tree to the one nearest her.

Mic shot at Robert. Robert ducked just in time to miss the bullet, which sent his hat flying off his head. Mic uttered a word she'd never heard before, and judging by the tone he used, she was better off not knowing.

She resisted the urge to look in Mic's direction. She had to keep her focus on Robert.

Robert lunged for her, and she braced herself. This time, a bullet hit his shoulder, but he didn't slow down. He made it to her, and before she had time to blink, he had his hand wrapped around her neck.

She swung the knife out from behind her back and stabbed him as hard as she could in his gut. Whether in shock or pain, he took a step back and stared at the knife lodged firmly in his stomach. A pool of blood quickly spread over his abdomen.

Then another bullet zoomed through the air and hit him in the side of the head. She let out a startled yelp and covered her eyes.

She heard Mic run up to her but was afraid to uncover her eyes until he reached her side and said that Robert was dead. On instinct, she wrapped her arms around Mic and buried her face in the side of his neck.

"It's alright," he whispered. "It's over. You're safe now."

"Robert brought Daniel and Wilson out here to get me," she said, noting the way her voice shook. "He wanted my trunk. He wanted the money I hid in it. I had no idea they followed me from Virginia. He paid Charles to lure me to the ranch, and Charles knew I'd come with you and the others. That's why Charles had most of his men leave for Denver with the cattle. It was all planned. We didn't take anyone by surprise." Realizing she was rambling, she stopped and took a deep breath.

"Yes, I know. I heard them talking when you and Robert were in the den with Charles."

Surprised, she looked at him. "You heard us? But how?"

"I saw you and Robert enter the house as Jeremiah and I were on our way to the spot we were supposed to meet you. I couldn't go without you, so Jeremiah created a diversion while I followed you two. I grew up in that house. I know all of the secret spots to hide. I had to stay back and wait for a bit, but I knew they were going to take you back the way we came. Jeremiah went straight to the cabin while I followed you."

Knowing Mic had been there the whole time made the whole experience less frightening. She collapsed against him. "I should have stayed at the cabin like you wanted."

"If you had, Charles would have had his men follow us back to my cabin. At least this way, Charles didn't see the need to go with Robert. So, as much as I hate to admit it, it was for the best you went."

"Did you see what happened with Abby and Lloyd?"

"I know they ran off on the horse, but I lost track of what direction she took."

"Did you see Wade?"

He nodded. "He got shot, but it's not a serious wound. He'll live. He had Lloyd but gave him to Abby when he realized there was a woman in the house."

"That was Millie. She was the woman I came on the stagecoach with. Charles took her when he realized I wasn't there. It was dark and she didn't see me, but I know it was her. Do you think he hurt her?"

"I have no way of knowing what he did to her."

That didn't sound comforting. She wanted to ask him what he thought Charles might have done to her, but he didn't know. She didn't know. The only people who knew were Charles and Millie, and neither was around to ask.

"I think Wade took Millie back to his hideout," Mic said as he put his arm around her shoulders and led her away from Robert's body. "Whatever happened or didn't happen to her, she's better off now. We need to get to our cabin so Jeremiah can notify the marshal that there's a couple of men out here for him to collect. If Wilson is smart, he'll leave and never show his face around here again."

"I don't think he wanted to hurt me."

"That was obvious. It's why I didn't kill him. I think after all of this, he's decided money isn't worth dying for."

"It's never worth dying for," she muttered as they went to the horse Wilson had been riding. "I wish more people understood that."

"Maybe someday they will." He squeezed her shoulders. "You were smart, you know. I'm proud of you for making Robert think you were scared of the outlaws and then making those men go in circles. I'm surprised it took Robert so long to realize what you were doing. You passed that tree four times. Just wait until I tell Abby what happened."

"I don't know. Until I can wrestle a coyote to the ground with my bare hands or eat a rattlesnake raw, I don't think I can impress her."

"She doesn't eat rattlesnakes raw. Alright, there was one time, but there wasn't anything to cook it with. She said she'd rather eat grasshoppers than raw snake ever again."

Lillian grimaced.

They reached the horse, and Mic kissed her. "As long as you're with me, I'll make sure you eat good meals."

She laughed, and some of the tension she'd been feeling ever since last night finally eased. "Since you put it that way, I'll never leave your side."

He chuckled and helped her onto the horse. "Good because I want you to be with me forever."

As soon as he got into the saddle, she snuggled up to him. She closed her eyes, thankful she could finally go home.

Chapter Sixteen

Sunlight hit Mic's eyes. Even without opening them, he knew it was late in the morning. This was the second day since bringing Lillian back that he'd overslept. If he wasn't careful, this was going to become a habit. While he didn't regret staying up late into the night to make love to her, he needed to get to sleep earlier tonight.

He got up on his elbow so the sun was no longer in his eyes and looked down at Lillian who was safely tucked up against his side. He brushed the hair from her cheek and kissed her smooth skin.

From outside, he heard someone moving around. He got out of the bed and peered out the small window in the loft. He saw Jeremiah washing out a pot.

Mic hurried to get dressed. He was hoping Jeremiah would return and tell him what happened with the marshal.

"Where are you going?" Lillian asked.

He glanced at her as he put on his boots. "Jeremiah's back."

"Did he bring anyone with him?"

"It doesn't look like it. I only see him."

She didn't hide her disappointment.

He offered her a sympathetic smile. "I'll ask about Abby, Lloyd, Wade, and Millie when I talk to him." He went over to her and kissed her. "I'm sure they're fine. My guess is that Abby took Lloyd to Wade's hideout."

"But she was supposed to come here."

"Yes, but she knew you were with Robert. I think she changed her plans when he took you."

"You're probably right."

He gave her another kiss. "Abby knows where everyone is, and she knows how to take care of herself. I wouldn't worry about her."

When her expression relaxed, he felt better. Maybe it was wrong to lie, but the last thing he wanted to do was worry her. Yes, Abby knew how to take care of herself. She was a skilled fighter, and she was smart. But the territory was a large one, and it was easy to get lost.

"Take your time getting ready for the day," he told Lillian and then hurried down the ladder.

Jeremiah filled the pot with water. "You want some coffee?" he asked as Mic came outside.

"Sure." Mic sat next to him. "Did you find Robert and Daniel?"

"I did," Jeremiah said as he set the pot over the small fire. "They were where you said they'd be. I even found Wilson."

Mic's eyebrows rose in surprise. "You did?"

He chuckled. "He ran straight for a preacher and confessed his sins. The preacher said before he took care of the sin problem, he had to get him to a doctor first. That bullet you shot was still in his arm."

"I had to get him to drop his gun somehow, but I didn't want to kill him."

"You did a fine job. Your pa would be proud you turned out to be such a good shot."

"You have to take part of the credit. You were helping me right along with him."

He shrugged. "I'm ten years older than you. What was I supposed to do? Stand by while you made pitiful attempts to hit your target? I figured you might as well learn from the best."

"It's nice to know you took your vow of humility seriously when you became a preacher."

Jeremiah shot him an amused grin. "At least everyone's alright. I wasn't sure what was going to happen when Lillian let out that whistle while we were still in the house. I thought we were goners."

"No. Not yet." And hopefully not ever where Charles was concerned. "I don't suppose the marshal is going to do anything to Charles for keeping a two-year-old from his father."

Jeremiah turned serious. "You know how things work around here. Things aren't going to be that simple. Wade isn't going to get that ranch back any time soon. The only reason the marshal took care of the men who kidnapped Lillian is because they're outsiders."

Mic was afraid of that, but he had to ask. It would've been nice if they could have rescued Lloyd and Lillian and managed to get Charles thrown into jail at the same time. But apparently, it wasn't going to be that easy.

"Charles let us take Lloyd," Mic said. "If he didn't want us to have Lloyd, he would have stopped us."

"Maybe. Maybe not. It's hard to know what really happened. We wounded a couple of his men, and he didn't have enough on the land to protect everything he had. It's possible that Lillian being there was enough of a distraction that allowed us to get Lloyd out of there."

"I heard him talking to Lillian. He said he let Lloyd go."

"That's what he said. It doesn't mean it's the truth."

Jeremiah had a point. Charles wasn't exactly known for his honesty.

"There is one thing I noticed, though," Jeremiah continued, a thoughtful tone in his voice. "While you were paying attention to what was going on with Lillian, I saw Wade and that woman making their way out of the house. One of Charles' men had a clear shot of him. He was ready to take it, but another whispered that Charles had ordered them to only wound Wade." Jeremiah looked at Mic. "He doesn't want Wade dead."

Of all of them, Charles hated Wade the most. Mic didn't know the details, but he knew the feud had been going on between them since he was a child. He couldn't recall a day when they ever got along.

"Maybe Charles wants Wade to live so he can watch him suffer," Jeremiah softly said. "Some men are like that. One would like to think that mankind isn't capable of that kind of evil, but such evil does exist."

Mic inwardly shivered. What a terrible thing it would be to have someone who actually enjoyed watching you suffer. "We have to get that ranch back, Jeremiah. We can't let Charles get away with this."

"We won't. The day will come when Charles will get what he deserves. But we need to be careful and wait until the time is right. We can't afford to rush things."

"I know." It was why he waited to take care of Robert, Daniel, and Wilson. "I don't act in haste like I did when I was a child."

"I figured that since you have Lillian back safe and sound."

After a few moments, Mic said, "I assume the others are alright since you haven't mentioned them."

"Wade's back at his little shack with that woman he rescued, but we haven't seen Abby or Lloyd," Jeremiah replied.

Picking up on the hesitation in his friend's voice, Mic asked, "Are you worried about Abby and Lloyd?"

"I'm sure they're fine," Jeremiah slowly said in a tone that indicated he didn't feel as confident as he wanted to be. "Something probably prompted her not to come here."

"Yeah. I told Lillian she saw Robert and the other two men taking her in this direction. Abby probably decided to go straight for Wade's instead. She wouldn't want to put the boy in harm's way."

"No, she wouldn't have."

But she hadn't been at Wade's when Jeremiah checked on him. So what, exactly, did that mean?

"I'm sure in a few days, Lloyd will be reunited with his pa," Jeremiah said, as if he was trying to convince himself everything would be fine. "Abby knows this territory as well as we do. She can find her way anywhere."

Could she? It was a large territory. If she ended up going in the wrong direction, she could end up getting lost.

"I suppose I can make the trip back to Wade's and see if they're there," Jeremiah said after a long pause.

"I think that would be a good idea. I'm sure everything's fine, but Lillian's worried. I think it'd be nice if she knew for sure that everyone's alright. And I'm sure she'd like to know how Millie is since Millie was in the stagecoach with her. Millie was that woman Wade rescued."

Jeremiah nodded. "I'll leave later today for Wade's hideout. Then I'll come back and let you know what's going on."

Mic breathed a sigh of relief. Good. He'd feel better if he knew that Abby and Lloyd were with Wade, and, as he'd said, Lillian would like to know how Millie was doing.

Jeremiah took the pot from the fire and poured coffee into a tin cup. He rummaged through his leather sack. "I think I got another cup in here."

"If not, I can get one from the house."

Mic got ready to stand up when Jeremiah pulled another cup out. With a grin, he said, "Always be prepared. That's what I say." He poured Mic a cup and handed it to him. He put the pot aside and sat back down. "How's married life treating you?"

"Good. I'm glad Lillian's here. It's nice to have someone else around this place, and, it's even better that I can make love to her."

Jeremiah chuckled. "I could tell you were eager to get to that part of the marriage as soon as she agreed to marry you."

Though Mic was well aware that Jeremiah and Wade had known what had been on his mind that day, he opted to drink the coffee instead of respond.

They sat in silence for a couple of minutes when the door of the cabin opened. Mic glanced over as Lillian came out with a tray that had two bowls on it.

"I thought you two might like something to eat." She came up to them and showed them the oatmeal. "It's nothing fancy, but it's hot."

"It's plenty fancy," Mic said as he took his bowl. "You added fruit to it."

"I thought some fruit would give it some flavor," she replied as Jeremiah took his bowl. "I couldn't find any sugar to sweeten it up."

Sugar was one of the things Mic missed ever since being stranded out here. "The last time Abby came with sugar was a year ago, if I remember right. The girl doesn't like to make trips to the general store. She'd rather be where the action is."

"That's Abby for you." Jeremiah chuckled and took a bite of the oatmeal. "This is good. I like the fruit. It's a nice touch."

After Mic finished swallowing his spoonful, he nodded his agreement. "It is good. Why don't you join us?"

"Oh, I don't want to intrude," she said.

"You're not intruding," Mic assured her. "You're part of the family. You belong out here with us." He pointed to Jeremiah. "He's been hanging around Wade for so long that he's like another brother. You're better because you're my wife."

Jeremiah snorted. "Thanks a lot."

Mic laughed. "It's so easy to rile you up." Turning back to Lillian, he said, "I'll get a chair. Get your bowl and come out here."

Jeremiah smiled at her. "You're more than welcome to join us any time you want."

Looking pleased, Lillian returned to the cabin, and Mic hurried to get her a chair.

When she returned to them, Jeremiah poured her a cup of coffee, and the three went on to have a pleasant conversation for her sake. Neither one wanted to worry her. In unspoken agreement, they had decided they would keep their concerns to themselves. Lillian wasn't like Abby. She was more delicate, and given her sensibilities, there was no point in giving her any bad news unless they knew something bad had happened.

Mic leaned close to her and gave her a kiss. The territory was a wild one. Anything could happen. But Abby had been well-trained, and that gave him hope all would be fine.

In the meantime, he would do his part to keep training Lillian how to defend herself. Whatever happened, he was determined that Lillian would never have to be as vulnerable as she'd been with Robert again. He might not be able to do anything about Abby, but he could do something about Lillian, and for the time being, that was going to have to be enough.

Books Coming Up in the Wyoming Series:

<u>The Rancher's Bride (Book 2)</u>: Abigail (Abby) learned early in life that you keep your secrets. Don't tell anyone anything unless you absolutely have to. This is good protection for you and for them. She's about to find out how hard it is to stick to that rule when she stumbles across the man of her dreams.

<u>The Fugitive's Bride (Book 3)</u>: Wade Gray marries a woman in order to give his son a mother who can continue to care for him in case he ends up dying when he goes to reclaim the family ranch. But it isn't long before he realizes his mistake. He never should have picked a woman who threatens to make him fall in love with her. Love is weakness, and if there's one thing he can't afford to be, it's weak.

***

If you would like to receive emails when these books—and other books I write—come out, sign up for my email list. https://ruthannnordinauthorblog.com/sign-up-for-email-list/

All Books by Ruth Ann Nordin
(Chronological Order)

Regencies

<u>Marriage by Scandal Series</u>
The Earl's Inconvenient Wife
A Most Unsuitable Earl
His Reluctant Lady
The Earl's Scandalous Wife

<u>Marriage by Design Series</u>
Breaking the Rules – coming soon
Nobody's Fool – coming soon

<u>Standalone Regency</u>
Her Counterfeit Husband (happens during A Most Unsuitable Earl)

<u>Marriage by Deceit Series</u>
The Earl's Secret Bargain
Love Lessons With the Duke
Ruined by the Earl
The Earl's Stolen Bride

<u>Marriage by Arrangement Series</u>
His Wicked Lady
Her Devilish Marquess
The Earl's Wallflower Bride

<u>Marriage by Bargain Series</u>
The Viscount's Runaway Bride
The Rake's Vow
Taming The Viscountess
If It Takes A Scandal

Native American Romance Series
Restoring Hope
A Chance In Time
Brave Beginnings
Bound by Honor, Bound by Love

Virginia Series
An Unlikely Place for Love
The Cold Wife
An Inconvenient Marriage
Romancing Adrienne

Standalone Historical Western Romances
Falling In Love With Her Husband
Kent Ashton's Backstory
Catching Kent
His Convenient Wife
Meant To Be
The Mail Order Bride's Deception

Contemporary Romances

Omaha Series
With This Ring, I Thee Dread
What Nathan Wants
Just Good Friends

Across the Stars Series
Suddenly a Bride
Runaway Bride
His Abducted Bride

Standalone Contemporaries
Substitute Bride

Co-Authored Romances

Historical Romance Anthologies
Bride by Arrangement
A Groom's Promise

Thrillers

Return of the Aliens (Christian End-Times Novel)
Late One Night (flash fiction)
The Very True Legends of Ol' Man Wickleberry and his Demise
- Ink Slingers' Anthology

Fantasies

Enchanted Galaxy Series
A Royal Engagement
Royal Hearts
The Royal Pursuit
Royal Heiress

Nonfiction

Writing Tips Series
11 Tips for New Writers
The Emotionally Engaging Character

Lightning Source UK Ltd.
Milton Keynes UK
UKHW021040060223
416538UK00017B/2378